U0016937

讀李家同學英文 4

李家同◎著

Nick Hawkins（郝凱揚）◎翻譯　周正一◎解析

The Eavesdroppers
竊聽者

透過李家同簡潔而寓意深遠的文章，領略用英文表達中文故事的妙趣
鑰匙◎屋頂◎對數字正確的認識◎我的家
◎竊聽者◎紐特，你為什麼殺了我？

序

李家同

我真該謝謝郝凱揚先生將我的文章譯成了英文。這當然不是一件簡單的事情,但是我看了他的翻譯,我發現他的翻譯是絕對正確的,而且非常優美。外國人寫的小說,往往用字非常艱難。對一般人而言,都太難了。這本書比較容易,沒有用太難的字。郝先生是美國人,能做這件事情,充分展現他的中英文造詣很高,他一定是一位非常聰明的人。

這一本書最大的好處是有對英文的註解、也有練習,想學英文的年輕人可以從註解中學到很多英文的基本學問。

我在此給讀者一個建議:你不妨先看看中文文章,先不看英文的翻譯,然後試著將中文翻成英文,我相信你一定會覺得中翻英好困難。翻完以後,再去看郝先生的翻譯,相信你可以學到不少,也可以寫出越來越像外國人寫的句子。

我尤其希望讀者注意標點符號的用法。英文的標點符號是非常重要的,中文句子對標點符號的標準比較寬鬆,但英文絕對不行,一個標點符號用錯了,全句的結構就是錯了。讀者可以利用這個機會好好

地學會如何正確地下英文的標點符號。

另外，千萬要注意動詞的用法，如果你英文動詞沒有錯，你的英文就很厲害了。信不信由你，英文不好的人常常不會用現在完成式，可是這本書裡用了很多的現在完成式，你不妨仔細研究為什麼要用這種我們中國人所不熟悉的時態。

在英文句子裡，一定要有一個主詞和一個動詞，讀者不妨在每一個句子裡去找一下，主詞和動詞一定會存在。我們中國人有時會寫一個英文句子，但是句子中，主詞和動詞弄不清楚，以至於有的動詞沒有主詞。也就因為如此，凡是這種主詞和動詞關係不清楚的句子，意思也會弄不清楚。讀者如果覺得這些文章很容易懂，其實完全是因為每一個句子的主詞和動詞都很清楚的原因。

如果你有時不知道如何用英文表達你的想法，你應該知道，這是正常的事。多看這本書，對你一定有幫助。

看這本書的時候，再次建議你先看中文，立刻試譯，再參考英譯。這樣做，對你的英文作文會有很大的好處。

最後我謝謝周先生，他的註解使這本書生色不少。當然我也該謝謝聯經出版公司，我相信這本書的出版會有助於很多想學好英文的年輕人，這本書能夠順利出現，林載爵先生和何采嬪女士有很大的功勞，我在此謝謝他們。

起而行

郝凱揚

李家同令人敬佩的地方，不在於他淵博的學問，也不在於他虔誠的信仰。我之所以佩服他，是因為他將他的理想付諸行動。

眾人皆知，李教授信奉的是天主教，而且他以他的信仰為寫作的出發點。在台灣，即使把天主教、基督教和摩門教三大派基督徒的人數全部加起來，所佔的比例還不到人口的一成。那麼，一個天主教徒寫的書怎麼會在台灣的社會廣受歡迎呢？關鍵在於「付諸行動」四個字。

幾年前，我在台灣當過兩年的傳教士。當我問人家「你有什麼宗教信仰」時，最常聽到的一句話是「所有的宗教都是勸人為善」。其實我並非不知道，說這句話的用意是以較為委婉的口氣拒絕我，但這十一個字所蘊含的意義非常深遠。儒家的「仁義」、道家的「道」、佛教的「慈悲」、基督徒的「博愛」、甚至無神論的「倫理」，宗旨都不外乎教人把內在的善性發揮出來。然而光說好聽的話沒有用——真正的信徒一定要實踐他的信仰，否則他只是個偽善者。李家同主要不是個作者，乃是個「做者」：文作得少，事做得多。也就是因為如此，才有這麼多的讀者閱讀他的書，並從中得到感動。

「實踐」是個極為管用的通則,我們不妨想想它如何適用在語言的學習上。假如一個人(我們不說他是誰)訂了一年的美語雜誌,每個月固定讀一本上好的英文教材,但他從來不寫半個英文字,也不說半句英語,試問,他的英文能力會突飛猛進嗎?他對自己的英文能力會有很大的信心嗎?我再來做另一個假設:倘若另一個人(我們依然不說他是誰)買不起最好的英文教材,但他喜歡跟幾個不會中文的外國朋友見面,也喜歡寫英文日記或部落格,那麼英文會不會豐富他的人生?他會不會比較容易記住他所學的東西?

你自己比較像這兩個人中的哪一個?如果你的答案令你不滿,你要如何改變你學英文的方式?以我學中文的經驗來說,我覺得最重要的是給自己一個愛學的理由和非練習不可的環境。愛學的理由可以好玩(想唱美國的流行音樂);文雅(更能欣賞英國文學);不良(可以搭訕外國女生);實際(要跟國外的客戶做生意);無聊(愛挑布希總統的語病)等等,找出自己的理由應該不難。尋找非練習不可的環境對無法長期出國的人可能沒那麼容易,可是並非不可能──除了以上提過的,和不會中文的外國人交朋友以及利用網路寫英文部落格,還有別的方法。還有,在學會講英文的過程中,一定要多出一些難堪的錯,發現了之後笑一笑自己,因為這樣才算豁了出去。如果你因為怕出糗而只講最簡單的英文,怎麼會進步?你又不是沒聽過四聲不準的外國學生說「我恨矮台灣人」(我很愛台灣人)啦!

最後我想說,我絕對不是個隨隨便便的譯者──把這些精采的故事譯成傳神的英文花了我不少心思。目的只有一個──希望你能藉此體會到英文的樂趣!至於進步,我和解析者周正一先生只能提供好的資源──要不要好好利用,完全由你決定了。

編學相長

周正一

「讀李家同學英文」系列邁入第四輯了，這真是不得了的成就。參與其中的編寫，當然與有榮焉。

首先要承認，在進行句型和重點的解析過程中，時時會碰到瓶頸。在把原作和譯文讀過之後，我會開始尋找各級程度的讀者必須要了解的重點，之後開始絞盡腦汁，尋思怎麼進行解析說明，幫助讀者在看過解析之後，能留下鮮明且久遠的記憶。

其實英文的固定句型畢竟有限，從第一輯到第四輯一路讀來的讀者應會發現，有些句型重複出現了。但是這裡要強調的是，即使句型相同，英文的寫法仍有多種變化，解說的角度和方式也會有所不同。

另外，在編寫時，我並不刻意強調著重文法，以免產生不必要的畏懼感和排斥感。但對學習英文至關緊要，比如假設語氣，那當然無法避免。我會盡力根據多年教學英文的經驗，輔以實例解說，以期解惑。片（成）語反倒較令我頭痛，因為它就和生字一樣，沒啥道理可言。讓學習英語的人、尤其是初學者非常頭痛。

再者，在解析完每個重點後，無論是句型、文法或片語，我都會附上用心設計的小試身手，讓讀者在實作中進一步去體會驗證。

這是一本三合一的學習書，就原作來說，我們可以欣賞到李家同充滿人性關懷和無限想像的文章。流暢的譯文和每書所附的譯文朗讀CD可以把讀者的英文程度提昇到一個更高的層次。至於我所負責的解析，則是輔助句型片語或文法這些工具，期望讀者對作者譯者的文字有更深刻的了解。

欲學習英文有成，興趣是不可少的動力來源。打開這一系列的任何一輯，去欣賞它、了解它、學習它，一定會有意想不到的進步。有句話說，教學相長。然而從參與編寫的過程中，我體悟到一個心得，亦即豈只教學相長？從編寫中，我也學到許多——從故事中，學到開闊恢宏，光明清滌的人性；從譯文中，我更學到不少前所未知的英文。學無止境，凡用心走過的，都是成長，都是收穫。

最後用以下這句話和讀者共勉開卷有益。

A book well written is something more than a collection of hundreds of printed pages. It is a wealth of wisdom and a well of pleasure.

目次
CONTENTS

Keys

鑰匙

1-5 　　我服務的公司常常會為了表示熱心公益而捐錢給慈善機構,雖然捐得不多,可是老闆卻總要派人先去看一下這些慈善機構,這次老闆在考慮要不要捐錢給一個老人院,我是這個公司的總經理,就被派去參觀一下。

　　老人院在鄉下,一看就知道辦得很好,裡面的老人全是窮人,沒有親人照顧,當然也不交任何費用。老人院的支出全靠社會熱心人士的捐款,也有很多的義工來幫忙。

　　就在我四處張望的時候,一位在替老人餵食的中年人忽然叫我,「李家同」,我覺得他有點面善,可是怎麼樣也想不起來他是誰。這位中年人看到我的迷惘表情,索性自我介紹了,「你一定不認得我了,我是梅乾菜小姜。」

　　這一下我記起來了,小姜是我大學的同學,一位成天快快樂樂的小子。他好吃,而且特別喜歡梅乾菜扣肉,我們因此給他取了一個綽號「梅乾菜小姜」,他對這個綽號絲毫不在乎,覺得這個綽號很有趣。

CD1-2
◇ welfare (n.) 福利
◇ donate (v.) 捐(錢;血)
◇ charity (n.) 慈善機構
◇ contribution (n.) 捐款

◇ general manager 總經理
◇ rural area 鄉下(鄉村)地區
◇ expenditure (n.) 支出;開銷
◇ finance (v.) 以金錢補貼

In order to show its interest in the welfare of the community, the company I work for often donates money to charity. Although we don't donate very much, our boss still sends someone to check out each charity before donating. One time he was considering making a contribution to a rest home, and as general manager of the company, I was sent to take a look at the place.

1-5
CD1-1

The rest home was in a rural area; a glance was enough to tell it was very well run. The old folks inside were all poor people with no families to care for them. They didn't have to pay any fees, of course—the rest home's expenditures were financed completely by donations from kindhearted people, and many volunteers came to help out.

As I was looking around, a middle-aged man who was feeding the rest home's occupants suddenly called my name: "Lee Jia-Tong!" I thought he looked familiar, but for the life of me I couldn't figure out who he was. Seeing my perplexed expression, he went ahead and introduced himself: "You must not recognize me—I'm Little Mustard Jiang."

Hearing that jogged my memory. Little Jiang was my classmate in college; he was one of those guys who's always in a good mood. He loved to eat, and he particularly loved pork slices cooked with fermented mustard greens, so we nicknamed him "Little Mustard Jiang". He didn't mind a bit—in fact, he thought the name was funny.

◇ occupant (n.) 居住者
◇ perplexed (adj.) 困惑不解的
◇ pork slice 豬肉片
◇ fermented (adj.) 發酵的

　　小姜是一個普普通通的人,也沒有什麼驚心的言論。唯一和大家不同的是,他很喜歡替窮人服務,他三年級以後就住校外。有一次,他突然在他住的地方收容了一位流浪漢,本來是小姜跑到流浪漢睡覺的地方去照顧他,後來這位流浪漢生病了,小姜就將他帶到自己住的地方去,每天給他東西吃,可是病情越來越重,小姜慌了起來,我們幾個人終於找到一家醫院願意收容他,但最後也在醫院裡去世。

6-10　　小姜要替窮人服務,當然因為他的宗教信仰,奇怪的是他從不傳教,至少從來沒有向我們傳過教,可是我們都知道他信的是什麼教。

　　小姜念過研究所,當完兵以後,在一家電子公司做事,三年以後,他失蹤了,誰也弄不清楚他到哪裡去了,我知道他曾去過印度。這一失蹤,有十幾年之久。

　　小姜目前衣著非常地破舊,沒有襪子,一雙便宜的涼鞋。他看到我,高興得不得了,可是他一定要我等他工作完畢以後才能和我聊天。

◇ controversial (adj.) 有爭議(性)的
◇ junior year 大學三年級
◇ deteriorate (v.) 惡化
◇ panic (v.) 驚恐;恐慌
◇ proselytize (v.) (使)改變宗教信仰
◇ serve in the military 服兵役

Little Jiang was a very ordinary person; he had no controversial views on anything. The one thing that made him different from everyone else was that he loved serving the poor. He moved off campus his junior year, and once he startled us by letting a hobo move in with him. It turned out that Little Jiang had been going to the place where the hobo slept to take care of him, but then the hobo got sick, so Little Jiang took him in and fed him every day. His health continued to deteriorate, however, and Little Jiang started to panic. Finally, a few of us found a hospital that would take the hobo in, but he ended up dying in the hospital.

Of course, the service Little Jiang gave to the poor had a lot to do with his religious beliefs, but, strange to say, he never proselytized, or at least he never tried to proselytize with us. But we all knew what church he belonged to.

6-10

After finishing grad school and serving in the military, Little Jiang got a job at an electronics company. Three years later, he disappeared. No one knew exactly where he went, but I knew he had been to India. His disappearance lasted for more than a decade.

Now Little Jiang's clothes were old and ragged. He wore no socks, just a cheap pair of sandals. He was thrilled to see me, but he insisted that I'd have to wait till his work was finished before he could chat with me.

◇ decade(n.)十年
◇ ragged(adj.)襤褸的；破破爛爛的
◇ sandal(n.)涼鞋
◇ thrilled(adj.)興奮莫名的

　　等所有的老人吃過以後，小姜也吃飯了。我注意到他吃的是老人吃剩的飯和菜，心中正在納悶，老人院的負責人過來向我解釋：「李先生，姜修士參加的修會很特別，他們好像只吃別人剩下的菜飯，姜修士飯量很大，而且我們感到他很好吃，一再給他準備好的飯菜，他都拒絕，只有除夕在吃年夜飯的那一頓，他才會和我們大家一起吃，看到他一年一次的大吃大喝，平時只肯吃剩菜，我們都難過得不得了，可是一點辦法也沒有。」我想起小姜過去好吃的樣子，簡直不能相信這個吃剩飯菜的就是小姜。

　　小姜終於可以離開了，我們久別重逢，本來應該去找一家咖啡館聊天；可是我注意到小姜一副窮人的樣子，實在不知道該到哪裡才好。我說小姜像個窮人，不僅僅是說他穿得很普通，很多大學生不也是穿得破破爛爛嗎？奇怪的是，小姜變得黑黑壯壯的，說老實話，有點像在街上做粗活的，這副模樣我們該到哪家咖啡館去？

11-15　　小姜看到我的窘態，立刻想出一個辦法，我們到他住的地方去吹牛。

◇ leftovers (n.) 殘羹剩菜
◇ rest home 安養院
◇ monastic [məˋnæstɪk] order 修道會
◇ reunite (v.) 重聚；團圓
◇ separation (n.) 仳離；分別
◇ fancy clothes (n.) 美衣華服

After all the old people had finished eating, Little Jiang sat down to eat. I noticed that he only ate the leftovers from the old people's meal. As I was marveling at this, the rest home director walked over to me and explained: "Mr. Lee, Brother Jiang belongs to a unique monastic order; I think they're only allowed to eat other people's leftovers. He's a big eater, and we can tell that he loves to eat. We've prepared better food for him lots of times, but he always refuses it. New Year's Eve dinner is the only time he eats with the rest of us. When we see him at his annual feast and think of how he usually eats nothing but leftovers, we feel terrible, but there's nothing we can do about it." I thought of how much Little Jiang had always loved to eat, and I couldn't believe that the man eating leftovers in front of me was him.

Finally, Little Jiang left the table. As old friends reunited after a long separation, by all rights we should have gone to a coffee shop to chat. But seeing how poor Little Jiang looked, I really didn't know where we should go. When I say he looked like a poor man, I don't mean merely that he wasn't wearing fancy clothes—don't a lot of college students dress shabbily as well? What was remarkable was that he had grown dark and rough-looking—truth be told, he looked like a guy who did manual labor in the street. With him looking like that, to what café could we go?

Little Jiang realized my awkward predicament and promptly thought of a plan: we could head over to his place and shoot the breeze.

11-15

◇ shabbily(adv.)粗鄙地；寒酸地　　◇ manual labor 人力；勞力
◇ remarkable(adj.)引人注意的　　◇ predicament(n.)困境
◇ breeze(n.)本指「微風」，此處意為「天南地北地閒聊」

　　小姜住在台北市相當破的地方，我注意到他沒有用鑰匙就打開了門，顯然他的門沒有上鎖。小姜告訴我，他的修會有一個規矩，男修士住的地方必定不可加鎖，以保證這些修士一貧如洗。我一看小姜的住處，嚇了一跳，可以算得上現代化器具的只有一具小型收音機，和一個小型瓦斯爐，一個燈泡從屋頂上吊下來，電視機、電風扇、電冰箱、桌子和椅子都沒有。地上有被子和枕頭，看來小姜不會被凍壞。衛浴設備更是簡單得無以復加。

　　房間裡有一些祈禱的書，都放在地上。

　　小姜告訴我從來不會有人進來偷東西，可是仍有人會送些東西來，比方說今天就有人送他一包吃的。我打開一看是做三明治切下來的麵包皮，他們這種修士是不能吃整片麵包的，可是麵包店每天要切下大批麵包皮做三明治，小姜和他們約法三章，專門吃這些麵包皮。十幾年來，小姜沒有吃過任何一片整片的麵包。

　　我問他為什麼要如此刻苦？小姜說他過去常去服務窮人，總覺得和他們格格不入，有一種由上而下的感覺。虧得在印度，發現了這個修

◇ run-down（adj.）破敗的　　　　　◇ genuinely（adv.）真正地
◇ evidently（adv.）顯然地　　　　　◇ appliance（n.）用具

Little Jiang lived in a pretty run-down part of Taipei, and I noticed that he opened his door without a key—evidently he hadn't locked it. Little Jiang informed me that his order had a rule to ensure the monks were genuinely poor: under no circumstances were they allowed to have locks on the doors of their houses. I took one look inside Little Jiang's house and was shocked to find that the only modern appliances he had were a small radio and a small gas stove. A light bulb hung from the ceiling. There was no television, electric fan, refrigerator, or table and chairs. On the floor there was a blanket and a pillow—at least it looked like Little Jiang wouldn't freeze to death. The bathroom, too, could not have been more austerely furnished.

There were some prayer books in the bedroom, all lying on the floor.

Little Jiang told me that no one had ever stolen anything from him, but there were a few people who gave him things. For example, today someone had given him a sack full of food. I opened it and found that it was filled with bread crusts cut off from sandwich bread. Monks of Little Jiang's order weren't allowed to eat whole slices of bread, but since bakeries would cut off piles of crusts from the bread they used to make sandwiches every day, they took to giving them to Little Jiang to eat. He hadn't had a whole piece of bread in over ten years.

I asked him why he had to be so ascetic. He replied that when

---

◇ austerely [ɔsˋtɪrlɪ] (adv.) 儉樸地；因陋就簡地
◇ prayer book 祈禱書；禱告經文
◇ bread crust 麵包屑
◇ bakery (n.) 西點麵包店；烘焙坊
◇ ascetic [əˋsɛtɪk] (adj.) 苦行的；禁慾的

　　會，他們不僅要服務窮人，也要使自己變成窮人，自從他參加了這個修會以後，他的服務工作順利多了。他說他過去替窮苦老人洗澡的時候，常覺得不自然，現在已經完全沒有這種感覺了。

16-20　　我忍不住問他會不會很想吃梅乾扣肉？他說他豈只常想而已，他還常常夢到有梅乾菜扣肉吃，醒來慚愧不止。可是也因為如此，他的「刻苦」才有意義，如果七情六慾都沒有了，這都不是犧牲了。

　　他還說了一些我聽不懂的道理，好像是說他在替世界上所有人類犯的罪做補償。人類越有人做壞事，他就越要做得刻苦。說實話，我不太懂這是怎麼一回事，可是我了解他的一切作法是根據他的宗教，他一定相信人類的壞事加起來以後，會被他的犧牲所抵銷掉。

　　小姜告訴我他曾經去山地住過整整一年，這也就是他皮膚變黑而且體格變壯的緣故，這一年下來，他的樣子很像窮人了，可是他很坦白

◇ condescend (v.) 降格屈就；紆尊降貴；帶著優越感表示親切
◇ crave (v.) 渴求
◇ precisely (adv.) 剛好；正好
◇ sensory pleasure 官能之樂
◇ abstain (v.) 戒絕

he had served the poor in the past, he didn't fit in with them, and he felt like he was being condescending. Fortunately, he discovered a monastic order in India whose members not only served the poor but became poor themselves. Ever since he joined the order, his work of serving had gone much more smoothly. Before, he said, he felt awkward when he helped elderly people bathe themselves, but now he didn't feel that way at all.

I couldn't resist asking him whether he was dying to eat some pork 16-20 with fermented mustard greens. He said that not only did he crave it constantly, but oftentimes he'd dream of eating it and then wake up feeling overwhelmed with shame. But it was precisely because of this that his "asceticism" had meaning—if he had no desire for sensory pleasures, abstaining from them wouldn't be a sacrifice.

He went on to say some things I didn't fully comprehend, something to the effect that he was helping to make reparation for the sins of the world: the more sins people committed, the more ascetically he had to live. Frankly, I didn't really understand the idea, but I did know that everything he was doing was based on his religion. He must have believed that his sacrifice could somehow compensate for the sum of all human wrongdoing.

Little Jiang also told me he had spent a year living in the mountains, which was why his skin had gotten darker and his physique bulkier;

◇ comprehend (v.) 理解
◇ reparation (n.) 修補；彌補
◇ commit (v.) 做（錯事等）；犯下

◇ compensate (v.) 補償
◇ physique [fɪˋzik] (n.) 體格

地告訴我，他畢竟不是生下來就是窮人，因此有時候仍有些有錢人的想法，比方說，每次走過網球場，就想進去痛痛快快打一場網球，可是他沒有襪子，沒有球鞋，更沒有球拍。而且由於他一再告訴自己是個窮人，因此一直沒有打過網球。

小姜還告訴我一件事，他在這十幾年內，事實上曾吃到兩塊梅乾菜扣肉，他當場吃了三大碗飯，也永遠忘不了吃梅乾菜扣肉的年月日。

我發現小姜仍是小姜，一點也沒有變，仍是個嘻嘻哈哈快快樂樂的小子。他告訴我，他不敢和老朋友聯絡，怕大家可憐他，可是每晚必定為我們祈禱，他也問了我的情形，發現我的事業不錯，衷心地替我高興。自始至終，小姜沒有任何一種自以為特別的表情，更沒有一點暗示我庸俗的意思。

21-25　　我和小姜殷殷道別，他要趕去替流浪漢服務，我識相地不用我的豪華轎車送他，畢竟他已非常不習慣乘坐私人汽車了。

◇ tennis court 網球場
◇ tennis match 網球賽
◇ racket (n.)（桌球；網球；回力球）球拍
◇ happy-go-lucky (adj.) 樂天知命的
◇ inferior (adj.) 較差的；較劣的
◇ reluctantly (adv.) 勉強地；百般不願地

after that, he looked just like a poor man. He did admit to me, though, that because he hadn't been born poor, he still sometimes thought like a rich man. For example, every time he walked past a tennis court, he would want to go in and enjoy a good old-fashioned tennis match. But he had no socks or tennis shoes, and no racket, either. Because he kept telling himself he was a poor man, he had never played another game of tennis.

There was one other thing Little Jiang told me: during his ten-plus years as a monk, there was one meal where he actually got to eat two slices of pork cooked with fermented mustard greens, along with three big bowls of rice. He said he'd never forget the day, month and year of that meal.

I realized Little Jiang hadn't changed a bit—he was the same happy-go-lucky guy he'd always been. He told me he hadn't gotten back in touch with his old friends because he was afraid we'd pity him, but he prayed for us every night. He asked me how I'd been doing, and when he found out that my career was going well, he was genuinely happy for me. From beginning to end, he never gave the slightest impression of self-righteousness, and he never hinted that I was somehow inferior.

At last, I reluctantly said goodbye to Little Jiang, as it was time for 　21-25
him to go serve the homeless. In deference to his feelings, I didn't offer to take him there in my luxury sedan—it would surely have made him uncomfortable to ride in a private car.

◇ deference [ˈdɛfərəns] (n.) 尊重；敬意　　◇ luxury sedan [sɪˈdæn] 豪華轎車

　　我要找汽車的鑰匙，偏偏拿出了一大堆別的鑰匙。到最後才拿出車子的鑰匙，小姜站在旁邊看到我一串一串的鑰匙拿出來，覺得好有趣，他拍了一下我的肩膀，「小李，搞什麼名堂，怎麼會有這麼多的鑰匙？」

　　小姜走了以後，我站在街上發呆。我的確擁有好多鑰匙，這些鑰匙都代表我的社會地位。

　　比方說，我的車鑰匙鍍了一種特別的金屬，上面還刻了我的名字，我打高爾夫球的俱樂部裡，特別給我一把鑰匙，表示我是他們的特級會員，可以使用他們的貴賓室。我做了總經理以後，又拿到了一把總經理專用洗手間的鑰匙。我知道美國有些大亨還有自己的電梯，可惜台灣不興這一套，否則我又可以多一把鑰匙。

　　小姜呢？他一把鑰匙也沒有，可是如果今夜他出了車禍，天使一定會從天降下，將一把開啟天國之門的鑰匙給他。

　　我擁有這麼多足以讓我炫耀自己社會地位的鑰匙，可就缺了這最重要的一把。

◇ amused（adj.）開心的；愉快的
◇ represent（v.）代表；表示
◇ engrave（v.）鑴刻

◇ preferred member 專屬會員
◇ VIP lounge 貴賓室
◇ tycoon（n.）大亨；大老闆

When I reached for my car keys, I had the bad luck to pull out a whole bunch of other keys first. Little Jiang was amused as he stood by watching me pull out ring after ring of keys. He patted me on the shoulder and said, "Little Lee, what's the deal? Why on earth do you have so many keys?"

After Little Jiang left, I stood there in the street, lost in thought. It was true I had an awful lot of keys—they represented my place in society. For instance, my car key was plated with a special kind of metal and engraved with my name. The club where I played golf had given me a key that meant that I was a preferred member and could therefore use their VIP lounge. When I became general manager, I got a key to my own private bathroom. There were even some American tycoons, I knew, who had their own elevators—it was a pity the practice hadn't yet caught on in Taiwan, or I'd have yet another key.

But Little Jiang? He didn't have a single key of his own. But if he happened to be killed in an accident tonight, surely angels would descend from the skies and give him a key to the gate of Heaven.

I had all these keys to show off my social status, but that one—the most important key of all—was conspicuously missing.

◇ elevator (n.) 電梯 (指升降梯)
◇ descend (v.) 下降
◇ social status 社會地位
◇ conspicuously (adv.) 明顯地；顯著地

（1）donate money to charity 捐款行善；捐款做慈善工作（1段）

In order to show its interest in the welfare of the community, the company I work for often donates money to charity.

我服務的公司常為了表示熱心公益而捐錢給慈善機構。

解析

其實這並非句型，也非片語。為什麼還把它挑出來作為重點呢？理由是它太實用、太生活化了。donate 為「捐贈」的意思，即使是「捐」血也是用這個字。「我每隔一個月捐血一次。」英文就表示為：I donate blood every other month. 請注意，donate 的名詞為 donor。整個 donate money to charity 的基本含意是「把金錢捐贈給慈善機構（charitable organization）」。另外提醒讀者們注意譯者怎麼處理「熱心公益」，譯者用 interest 表達「熱心」，用 the welfare of the community 表達「公益」，看來簡單，實則不易。

小試身手

1.　她將薪水的五分之一捐給慈善團體。

　　＿＿＿＿＿＿＿＿＿＿＿＿＿＿＿＿＿＿＿＿＿＿＿

（2）check out 查個清楚；徹底了解（1段）

Although we don't donate very much, our boss still sends someone to check out each charity before donating.

雖然捐得不多，可是老闆卻總要派人先去看一下這些慈善機構。

解析

check out 強調把有關某人某事的相關背景資料查個徹底仔細。英文另有個片語 check up on 在用法和意義上與 check out 極為接近。順便介紹一個由 although 引導的（讓步）副詞子句：although we don't donate very much。讀者可透過中英對照閱讀而知道 although 的意思為「雖然」，請特別

記得，它是個從屬連接詞，它的後面跟著一個子句，而整個就稱之為「讓步副詞子句」，和另外的「主要子句」共同組成一個「句子」。現在我們實際看一個例子：

（1）他起床得早。

He got up early.

（2）他沒能趕上火車。

He failed to catch the train.

（雖然）他起床得早，他沒能趕上火車。

Although（1）＋（2）.

→ Although he got up early, he failed to catch the train.

小試身手

2. 因為水管似乎是漏水的源頭，他決定檢查一下。

_____

（3）**a glance was enough to tell...** 看一眼就夠……；一望而知……（2段）

The rest home was in a rural area; a glance was enough to tell it was very well run.

老人院在鄉下，一看就知道辦得很好。

解析

a glance is enough to tell... 這個用語簡直和中文的「一望而知」語意完全相同。一西一中，竟然雷同到直如一個模子印出來的，也算是罕見。既然如此，tell 在這裡就不是一般所見作「告訴」解釋，而是當作「區別分辨」、

「看得出來」解釋。你的同事今天在辦公室,哈欠連連,睡眼惺忪,你就跟他說:「一看就知道你昨晚沒睡好。」假設你的同事是老外,該怎麼用英文告訴他呢?

小試身手

3. 一看就知道你昨晚沒睡好。

_____

(4) for the life of me 再怎樣也(不);打死(我)也(不)(3段)

I thought he looked familiar, but for the life of me I couldn't figure out who he was.

我覺得他有點面善,可是怎麼樣也想不起來他是誰。

解析

某人「有點面善」、「看起來面熟」,形容詞即表示「面善」、「面熟」,因此「看起來面熟」,英文即為 look familiar。另一個要點為 for the life of me,本意為「打死我也(不)」,在引申的用法裡就是「再怎樣也(不)」。這裡當然是個誇飾法,帶點幽默的語氣,表示怎麼樣都想不起或弄不清楚,並非真的會危害到性命的行為。

小試身手

4. 那本書的名字,無論我怎麼挖空心思都想不起來!

_____

(5) 文法要點：分詞構句 Ving..., S＋V＋ ...（3段）

Seeing my perplexed expression, he went ahead and introduced himself: "I'm Little Mustard Jiang."

這位中年人看到我的迷惘表情，索性自我介紹了，「你一定不認得我了，我是梅乾菜小姜。」

解析

把英譯和句型對比，就可以發現句子的結構為：Ving..., S＋V＋ ...。這個置於主詞與動詞之前的 Ving...，文法上稱之為「分詞構句」，多半為現在分詞（Ving），但過去分詞（Vpp）亦有可能，而且不乏其例。讀者務必要注意的是，這個分詞構句和其後句子的主體（即 S＋V＋ ...）有絕對密切的關係。我們用以下實例來幫讀者了解。

兩個部份：知道時間所剩無幾　　　　我們加快腳步
knew there wasn't much time left　　we quickened our steps

請問讀者，你說「知道時間所剩無幾」和「我們加快腳步」有沒有關係呢？當然有，腳步之所以加快，是因為時間所剩無幾。這就是兩者間的關係。

現在我們把這兩部份併成一個句子，其結果為：
Knowing there wasn't much time left, we quickened our steps.

以上句子中的 knowing there wasn't much time left 即是「分詞構句」，你瞧，它和英譯 seeing my perplexed expression 很一致吧（註：在此指的是開頭 Ving 的部份）。

小試身手

5. 她把自己丟在床上，無法控制地哭泣。

_____

（6）jog one's memory 使……回想起來（4段）

Hearing that jogged my memory.
這一下我記起來了。

解析

一看到 jog，不少人就先入為主地往「慢跑」的方向想。可是在以上的句子裡，任你再怎麼硬拗，也不可能用「慢跑」的字義把句子拗出一個過得去的解釋。所以，在學習英文的過程中，有時還不能太過於先入為主。這裡給各位的忠告是：一覺得不對勁，趕緊拿出字典來查，不要一直抱殘守缺，緊抓著過去所學關於某個字的定義不放。

動手查字典，字典就會告訴你，jog 除了「慢跑」，還具有「觸動；喚起（記憶）」，「使某人回憶起（已經遺忘的）某事」的意義。

小試身手

6. 一開始我記不得他是誰，但聽了他的聲音我就想起來。

_____

（7）It turns out that... 原來（是）……（5段）

It turned out that Little Jiang had been going to the place where the hobo slept to take care of him…
本來是小姜跑到流浪漢睡覺的地方去照顧他……

解析

這的的確確是個句型，要花些心思去體會，它的意思相當於中文的「原來（是）……」。也就是說，本來某個事情的來龍去脈搞不清楚，後來事情的輪廓慢慢浮現出來，事情的梗概變得鮮明活現。比方中文說：「搞了半天原來他和一群朋友在咖啡廳聚會。」英文可以說：It turned out that he was hanging out with a bunch of friends at a café.

小試身手

7. 原來冥王星太小了，不能稱為行星。

_____

(8) someone ends up Ving... 最後……；後來……（5段）

Finally, a few of us found a hospital that would take the hobo in, but he ended up dying in the hospital.

我們幾個人終於找到一家醫院願意收容他，但最後也在醫院裡去世。

解析

動詞 end 本身就具有「結束；終了」，後面再接個介副詞 up 更加重「一切到此終結」的意思。學習這個片語（句型）最重要的是後面若是動詞時，要使用動名詞（Ving），以英譯為例即是 dying。

小試身手

8. 我們本來打算去野餐，可是下雨了，所以我們後來改看電影。

_____

(9) have a lot to do with... 和……很有關係（6段）

strange to say 說也奇怪

Of course, the service Little Jiang gave to the poor had a lot to do with his religious beliefs, but, strange to say, he never proselytized, or at least he never tried to proselytize with us.

小姜要替窮人服務，當然因為他的宗教信仰，奇怪的是他從不傳教，至少從來沒有向我們傳過教。

解析

本句英譯裡，撇開生字不論，讀者們至少有兩樣東西可學。一個為 have a lot to do with...，每個字都很簡單，可是組合起來卻讓初見識的人摸不著頭腦，其實它指的是「和……非常相關」、「和……很有關係」這方面的意思。若講到「和……無關／沒什麼關係」，則使用 have nothing/little to do with...。若是「和……略有關係」，則使用 have something to do with...。另一個可學東西是 strange to say，從字面很容易就可以記住它的意思「說也奇怪」，表示說話者對之後的敘述（就英譯言就是 he never proselytized）所持的態度。你對這種用法陌生嗎？其實學過幾年英文的人應該不致於吧。sad to say, needless to say, shameful to say 這類片語你該見過一兩個吧。

小試身手

9. 我和那火災一點都沒關係。

_____

---

(10) a big eater 食量大；很能吃（9段）

He's a big eater, and we can tell that he loves to eat.
姜修士飯量很大，而且我們感到他很好吃。

解析

英文常有這種用名詞表示動作的情形。比如，用 a good swimmer 來表示「很會游泳／泳技高超」，用 a good dancer 來表示「舞跳得很好」，a good writer 表示「很會寫書」，而 a good student 當然就是「很會讀書」、「書讀得很好」的意思。當然要表示這些游泳、跳舞、寫作、讀書的技能很「彆腳」，可以把形容詞 good 改為 lousy 就得了。從以上所舉的例子來看，讀者很容易可以推知 a big eater 為「飯量很大」、「很能吃」的意思了，如果食量不大，不是很能吃，那可以把 big 改為 modest，變成 a modest eater。

小試身手

10. 我以前很迷 Michael Jackson。

_____

（11）There's nothing we can do about it. 沒辦法；無可奈何（9段）

...we feel terrible, but there's nothing we can do about it.

……我們都難過得不得了，可是一點辦法也沒有。

解析

本書從第一輯到現在這第四輯，很少把整個句子列成一個重點的，而這裡就是。There's nothing we can do about it. 實在是一句很實用的口語，中外皆然。難題當前，實在拿不出辦法了，許多人會雙手一攤，嘴巴說句：「沒辦法。」當然，用被動的型態也很好，就把它放在小試身手裡，讀者好好思考一番。

小試身手

11. 看樣子已經沒辦法了。

_____

（12）what's remarkable is that... 值得注意的是……；值得一提的為……（10段）

truth be told 說真的

do manual labor 做粗活；從事勞力工作

What was remarkable was that he had grown dark and rough-looking—truth be told, he looked like a guy who did manual labor in the street.

奇怪的是，小姜變得黑黑壯壯的，說老實話，有點像在街上做粗活的。

解析

remarkable 的本意為「值得注意」、「值得一說」，因此利用它所形成的習慣語 what was remarkable was that... 就表達了「值得注意的是……」或「值得一提的為……」。例如以下這句話：「值得注意的是臭氧層的破洞雖然沒有擴大，但也沒有縮小。」該怎麼以英文表達呢？請在小試身手裡展現你的功力吧。接著讀者可以學習到 truth be told 這個用語。它是被動的形態，如果用主動的形態，那就是大家更常見的 to tell the truth，兩者都表達相當於中文的「說實在的」、「說真的」這方面的意思。最後，「做粗活」、「從事勞力性質的工作」，譯者以 do manual labor 來處理，精準無比。

小試身手

12. 值得注意的是臭氧層的破洞，雖然大小沒有擴大，卻也沒有縮小。

_____

---

(13) with someone looking like that 某人那個樣子（外貌；長相；德行）(10段)

With him looking like that, to what café could we go?
這副模樣我們該到哪家咖啡館去？

解析

你當然希望別人說你 look like an angel，不但外表喜樂甜美，而且心地仁慈善良，人見人愛。你大概不希望別人說你 look like a horse 或者 look like a clown ——前者其貌不揚，後者則是耍寶輕浮之輩。重點裡的 look like that「那個樣子」、「那個德行」，雖沒有明說尊容長相如何，但是貶損之意昭然若揭。其實，這句最最重要的是介詞 with 的用法。這個結構：with somebody Ving... 表達一種相當於中文「（以）某人……的樣子」的附帶狀況。with 還可與其他語詞連用，底下句子即是一例。

小試身手

13. 價格這麼便宜，你一定是瘋了才不好好把握機會。

_____

（14）shoot the breeze 天南地北瞎聊天；抬槓；擺龍門陣（11段）

We could head over to his place and shoot the breeze.
我們到他住的地方去吹牛。

解析

這句短短的英譯裡，有兩個值得一學的東西。第一個是 head over to，請注意 head 是動詞（註：你該注意到它的位置在助動詞 could 之後吧），意思為「往（某方向或地方）去」，因而 head over to 是「到某地方去」之意。另一個要點比較難以從字面抓得到意思，不少人，即使程度還不賴，看到 shoot the breeze 都不禁在頭腦裡打個大問號，這是什麼碗糕？其實這個用語跟大多數老外來到台灣突然聽到「打屁」（對不起，用了粗話）這兩個字時的反應一樣，摸不著頭緒，心裡會想說：What the hell does it mean? 所以，該硬記時只好低頭認了，好好把它記一記吧，shoot the breeze 就如中文，俗氣一點説叫「打屁」、「抬槓」、「扯淡」，文雅一點就是「天南地北閒聊」。

小試身手

14-1. 爺爺愛和他的老朋友打屁。

_____

14-2. 我們正要往山的另一側，這時一陣暴風雪襲來。

_____

(15) under no circumstances 絕對不 (12段)

...under no circumstances were they allowed to have locks on the doors of their houses.

……(他們)男修士住的地方必定不可加鎖。

解析

這是個重要的片語，除了意義重要，用法更是不可小覷。circumstance(s) 的本意是「情況」（常用複數形），所以 no circumstances 就成了「沒這狀況」，under no circumstances 語意是「不在這情況之下」，也就衍生出「絕對不」的意思來。

至於其用法更是重要。no 具備了「否定」（而且還是強烈否定）的意味，所以當它的位置被提到句子前面去來凸顯否定時，句子就必須「倒裝」。所以眼尖的讀者會發現，本來應該是 ... they were allowed... 變成了 ... were they allowed...。

以下小試身手裡有兩處空白，請在第一個空白填入非倒裝的句子，在第二個空白填入倒裝的句子。你也許會發現，因為你閱讀過以上的觀念解析，有了心得，所以做起第二處空白比較得心應手。

小試身手

15. 你絕對不該跟父母撒謊。

_____

（非倒裝）_____

（倒　裝）_____

（16）語法觀念：以比較級呈現最高級（12段）

The bathroom, too, could not have been more austerely furnished.

衛浴設備更是簡單得無以復加。

解析

用比較級可以呈現出最高級的意思嗎？看看中文就知道了。「鎮上沒有人比他更有錢了。」這句話該怎麼以英文表現呢？希望你的答案是：No one in the town is richer than him. 請注意這句英文使用了比較級（richer），但是你可否注意到這句話其實表達是「他是鎮上最有錢的。」以英文即：He is the richest man in town.

所以最高級的意思是可以用比較級來傳達的，但是有一個條件不能不注意，就是這比較級必須和「否定」合作，才能充份把最高級的意思表現出來。「這所學校人數最多。」不就等於說「沒有其它學校比這所學校人數更多」嗎？前者使用最高級而後者使用比較級，讀者就利用小試身手來揣摩其中的道理吧。

小試身手

16-1. 這所學校人數最多。

_____

16-2. 沒有其它學校比這所學校人數更多。

_____

（17）fit in with... 和（一群人）契合；投合（15段）

He replied that when he had served the poor in the past, he didn't fit in with them, and he felt like he was being condescending.

他（小姜）說他過去常去服務窮人，總覺得和他們格格不入，有一種由上

而下的感覺。

解析

掏錢買衣服時總得先到試衣間穿穿看，了解是不是合身。試衣間叫作 fitting room，所以現在回到這個片語 fit in with...，你就該有更深入的體會了吧。fit 有「適合」、「合身」的意思，「那件洋裝合身嗎？」以英文言就是 Does the dress fit you? 衣著要合身才舒服，所以，fit in with 這個片語就如衣服之於人，大小適度，兩者極為契合。引申指人的世界，自然就是指人在團體裡或環境裡，很能融入，很能和他人配合，沒有一點牴觸衝突，非常自在的狀態。

小試身手

17. 他是天性安靜的男孩，沒法子融入他嘈雜的班上同學。

_____

(18) cannot resist Ving... 又回復到老樣子（16段）

　　　(be) dying to V…

I couldn't resist asking him whether he was dying to eat some pork with fermented mustard greens.

我忍不住問他會不會很想吃梅乾扣肉？

解析

用 cannot resist Ving...「忍不住……」實在是恰到好處。就字面說，cannot resist 為「無法抗拒」的意思，「無法抗拒做某事」其實就等同「忍不住想做某事」。你有過類似如下的經驗嗎？非常想吃某種食物，想都想「死」了。人同此心，中外皆然。特別留意，這種用法的 dying 是如假包換的形容詞，意思是「非常渴望的」。

18. 我好想喝杯珍珠奶茶。（我想喝珍珠奶茶想死了。）

_____

（19）**feel overwhelmed with...** ……不堪；……難抑；……不得
　　了（**16段**）

He said that not only did he crave it constantly, but oftentimes he'd
dream of eating it and then wake up feeling overwhelmed with shame.
他說他豈只常想而已，他還常常夢到有梅乾菜扣肉吃，醒來慚愧不止。

解析

除了「慚愧不堪」還有什麼不堪、不得了的呢？想一想，原來還滿多的：「高
興得不得了」、「傷心得不得了」、「氣得不得了」。你大概已經發現到 be/feel
overwhelmed with，指的都是一些情緒方面的東西，表示這些情緒之大、之
強烈讓人難以負荷。以下的小試身手就姑且以這些「不得了」為內容吧。

小試身手

19. 高興得不得了　_____

　　傷心得不得了　_____

　　憂心得不得了　_____

　　氣得不得了　　_____

　　感恩得不得了　_____

(20) must have Vpp（過去）一定......（17段）

　　　compensate for... 補（抵）償......

He must have believed that his sacrifice could somehow compensate for the sum of all human wrongdoing.

他一定相信人類做的壞事加起來以後，會被他的犧牲所抵銷掉。

[解析]

首先介紹一個重要的文法觀念：對過去事情的肯定推測（must have Vpp）。念小學的弟弟從外面回來，渾身上下傷痕累累，你根據他的前科，不等他開口就搶著說：「你一定又是和別人打架了。」這樣的一句話是你個人對事情的肯定推測，說「肯定」，因為你的話裡有「一定」這兩個字眼，說「推測」則表示這是一種主觀研判，你並未親眼看到你弟弟打架，他也有可能不小心跌傷或撞傷。但是打架也好（可能性極大），跌傷撞傷也罷（可能性極小），都是「過去」的事情（你弟弟現在人不就在家裡嗎？）綜合以上的情況，英文就得以這個型態表達：must have Vpp...。所以「你一定是和別人打架了。」以英文表現應該如下：

You must have gotten into a fight again.

動詞片語 compensate for... 即是用來表示「彌補」不足或「補償」虧欠。法官常判某甲譭謗某人而要賠償某乙多少錢，如果你是這位某乙，會不會覺得：How can money compensate for a damaged reputation?

┌───┐
│ **小試身手**

20-1. 她英文說得那麼好！（她）一定是在國外受教育的。

_____

20-2. 他很棒的數學能力彌補了他拙劣的寫作技巧。

_____
└───┘

(21) one's career is going well 事業發展順利（20段）

...and when he found out that my career was going well, he was genuinely happy for me.

……發現我的事業不錯，衷心地替我高興。

解析

某人畢生致力從事的工作，無論是從政或是從商還是任公職，都算是他的 career，這個字中文一般以「事業」對應，似乎比較狹隘了些。go well 可以直接從字面看出是表示事情「進展順利」、「過得很好」。所以，one's career goes/ is going well 表示著某人從政、經商，或從事任何職業工作路途順利，甚至小有所成。

小試身手

21. 最近我們的研究項目進展得特別順利。

_____

(22) never give the slightest impression of... 一點……表情都沒有（20段）

From beginning to end, he never gave the slightest impression of self-righteousness, and he never hinted that I was somehow inferior.

自始至終，小姜沒有任何一種自以為特別的表情，更沒有一點暗示我平庸的意思。

解析

當想以英文表示「一點……表情都沒有」或「沒有／看不出……的神色」時，即可以使用 never give the slightest impression of...（或者 never show any sign of...）。impression 是「表情」、「神情」，而 slight 為「些微」、「輕微」。所以 the slightest impression 為「最些微最輕微的表情」，放在動詞

give 之後作 give 的受詞，而 give 在此片語裡為「散發」、「散放」之意。綜合起來，never give the slightest impression of... 就表示了「最輕微的……表情都沒有散發出來」。

另外，這裡的 self-righteous 意為「自以為比別人正義」，表示小姜不以為做善事就比較正確、比較清高。

小試身手

22. 我有個老闆對我不甚滿意的印象。

_____

(23) in deference to... 對……（表示）尊重（21段）

In deference to his feelings, I didn't offer to take him there in my luxury sedan....

我識相地不用我的豪華轎車送他……

解析

deference 為「尊重」、「敬重」的意思。所以片語 in deference to... 自然就是「對（某人）表示敬重」。別誤解了，譯者不是用 in deference to 來表現「識相」，而是以 in deference to his feelings「尊重他的感受」來處理，說來是很不錯的角度。否則「識相」的翻譯難度還顏高的。

小試身手

23. 雖然她很想成為音樂家，但為了滿足她父親的希望，她選擇了學醫。

_____

(24) what's the deal 這是幹嘛呀；搞什麼名堂(什麼鬼)(22段)
Why on earth... 到底為什麼……

"Little Lee, what's the deal? Why on earth do you have so many keys?"
「小李，搞什麼名堂，怎麼會有這麼多的鑰匙？」

解析

What's the deal? 實在是句常用的口語英文。用中文表現出它的神韻很不簡單，譯者用這句口語處理原著「搞什麼名堂」，真算得上恰到好處。當老美對你來一句 What's the deal? 時，往往就等於說「怎麼回事？」

英譯為了配合前面的 What's the deal?，特別在 why 的後面添加 on earth，再把語氣的強度築高（從 why「為什麼」到「到底是為什麼」why on earth）。

小試身手

24. 戴那個怪帽子幹麼？

_____

(25) lost in thought 陷入沉思；深思；發呆(23段)

After Little Jiang left, I stood there in the street, lost in thought.
小姜走後，我站在街上發呆。

解析

你也許曾經 get lost in a new city，也許曾經 get lost in the jungle，也許曾經 get lost in the pursuit of fame and wealth，也許言行讓他人受不了而乾脆請你 Get lost! 你當然也有可能因為經歷了某事而一時百感交集，千頭萬緒一齊湧至心頭。這就是 lost in thought 這個片語所描述的狀況吧，以致於對外在環境渾然不覺，旁人看了，還真覺得你在發呆哪。

小試身手

25. 她陷入沉思而沒聽到名字被喊到。

_____

(26) an awful lot of... 多（到一大堆）的……

It was true I had an awful lot of keys—they represented my place in society.

我的確擁有好多鑰匙，這些鑰匙都代表我的社會地位。

解析

a lot of... 是人人皆知的片語，如果在 lot 之前加個 awful 使之成為 an awful lot of...，當然還是表示「多」，但是感覺更真確、更具體，也就是它讓人感覺這個「多」是「一大堆的多」，感覺也口語多了。

小試身手

26. 你覺得還好嗎？你真的吃了一大堆火雞肉啊！

_____

(27) catch on 流行；跟進／上（23段）

...it was a pity the practice hadn't yet caught on in Taiwan, or I'd have yet another key.

可惜台灣不興這一套，否則我又可以多一把鑰匙。

解析

典型的英文成語，要直接從字面判斷意義，難如登天。不過把困難和沮喪擺一邊，用心思索，還是可以尋出些蛛絲馬跡。野炊烤肉，你負責生火，手忙

腳亂半天，火柴耗盡，打火機用光，煤炭還是著不了火，這個「著（不了）火」英文一般用（not）catch fire 來表達。所以，catch 就有了「著（了）」、「起（了）」的意思。別忘了介副詞 on 具有「持續」和「進行」的意味喔。因此，當我們想說某種時尚，某個觀念風行並大行其道，即可用 catch on 表示。

小試身手

27. 你知到DIY從何時開始風行的嗎？（註：DIY為「自己動手做」之意＝Do It Yourself）

_____

小試身手解答

1. She donates a fifth of her salary to charity.

2. Since the water pipe seemed to be the source of the leak, he decided to check it out.

3. A glance is enough to tell that you didn't sleep well last night.

4. I can't think of the name of that book for the life of me!

5. She threw herself on the bed, weeping uncontrollably.

6. At first I couldn't remember who he was, but hearing his voice jogged my memory.

7. It turns out that Pluto is too small to be called a planet.

8. We had planned to have a picnic, but it rained, so we ended up watching a movie instead.

9. I had (absolutely) nothing to do with that fire.

10. I used to be a big fan of Michael Jackson.

11. It looks like nothing can be done about it.

12. What's remarkable is that the hole in the ozone layer, though not increasing in size, is not shrinking either.

13. With prices so low, you'd be crazy not to take advantage!

14-1. Grandpa loves to shoot the breeze with his old buddies.

14-2. We were heading over to the other side of the mountain when a snowstorm struck.

15. You should not tell lies to your parents under any circumstances.

　　Under no circumstances should you tell lies to your parents.

16-1. This school has the greatest number of students.

16-2. No other school has a greater number of students than this one.

17. A quiet boy by nature, he didn't fit in with his noisy classmates.

18. I'm dying for a cup of pearl milk tea.

19. 高興得不得了 be overwhelmed with joy

　　傷心得不得了 be overwhelmed with grief

　　憂心得不得了 be overwhelmed with worry

　　氣得不得了 be overwhelmed with anger/fury

　　感恩得不得了 be overwhelmed with gratitude

20-1. She speaks English so well! She must have been educated abroad.

20-2. His great mathematical ability compensates for his poor writing skills.

21. Our research project has been going particularly well lately.

22. I get the impression that the boss isn't satisfied with me.

23. Although she wanted to be a musician, she chose to study medicine in deference to her father's wishes.

24. What's the deal with the funny hat?

25. She was so lost in thought that she didn't hear her name being called.

26. Are you feeling okay? You sure ate an awful lot of turkey!

27. Do you have any idea when DIY first caught on?

A Roof Over My Head
屋頂

1-5　　我這一輩子，只有一個願望，走進一間有屋頂的房子，睡在一張有床單的床上。

　　為什麼我有這種願望呢？因為我是印度加爾各答的一個小乞丐，我生下來不久，爸爸就去世了，我和媽媽相依為命，我們都是乞丐，住在一條小街上，爸爸去世以前，在街上弄到一塊木板，爸爸在木板上加了一塊塑膠布，木板斜靠在牆上，晚上我們兩人擠進去睡覺。下大雨的時候，我們仍然會被淋溼。可是我們已經是幸運的了，有的小孩子更可憐，他們沒有木板可以擋掉一部分的風雨，每天晚上完全露宿街頭，一下雨，就要四處找一個地方躲雨，弄得不好，還會被人趕。

　　媽媽告訴我，爸媽過去也有屋子住的，爸爸是個農人，可是接二連三的壞收成，爸爸先是失去了牛，然後失去了那一塊地，最後將唯一的小屋子也賣掉，換成了錢，步行到加爾各答來，不久我哥哥和姊姊陸續死去。爸爸做各種苦工，我生下以後，爸爸病死，媽媽只好求乞為生，我長大了以後也學會了求乞。

CD1-4
　◇ sheet (n.) 床單；被單
　◇ beggar (n.) 乞丐
　◇ plank (n.) (大片的) 木板
　◇ attach (v.) 附加；裝上
　◇ squeeze (v.) 擠壓；緊縮
　◇ board (n.) (大片的) 木板

For my whole life, I've had only one wish: to be able to go inside a house with a roof and sleep on a bed with sheets.

Why do I wish this? Because I'm a child beggar in Calcutta, India. Not long after I was born, my dad passed away. My mom and I relied on each other to survive. We were both beggars, living in an alley. Before Dad died, he got a wooden plank from the street, attached a sheet of plastic to it, and leaned it against the wall. At night, the two of us would squeeze inside to sleep. If it rained hard, we'd still get wet, but we were lucky to have what we had. Some kids had it worse—they had no boards to block out the wind and rain. Every night they slept unsheltered in the open street. Whenever it started to rain, they'd have to search frantically for a place to take cover, and on a bad night, they might not find one where they wouldn't be driven away.

Mom told me that she and Dad used to have a house to live in. Dad had been a farmer, but a string of bad harvests made him lose first his ox and then his land. Finally he had to sell all he had left—his little house—for cash and walk to Calcutta. Soon after, my older brother and sister died, one after the other. Dad slaved away as a manual laborer until he got sick after I was born and Mom was forced to beg for a living. When I grew up, I too learned to beg.

◇ unsheltered(adj.)無所遮蔽的
◇ frantically(adv.)情急地；慌亂地
◇ harvest(n.)收成；收穫
◇ slave(v.)做苦工；做粗活
◇ manual laborer(n.)勞力工作者

　　我運氣很好，可以在歐貝利爾大旅館前面求乞，這是加爾各答最大的旅館，門口的人行道極寬，上面有頂，沿街有極粗的白色柱子，整個旅館當然也是白色的，漂亮極了。雖然旅館客人喜歡坐汽車進出，還是有不少旅客會出來走走，因為沿街有些賣書報的攤子，他們來買報紙，我就趁機上前去求乞，我發現東方面孔的旅客特別慷慨，我們乞丐一天通常可以要到十個盧比（五角美金），有一次一位東方的旅客給了我五十塊盧比。

　　可是媽媽也離我去了。三個月前，她病了，越病越嚴重，我用我們所有的錢設法買些好的食物給她吃，也沒有用。最後她告訴我，德蕾莎修女創立了一個垂死之家，她如果能被人送到那裡去，會有人照顧她，也可能會好，如果病好了，她會回來找我。

6-10　　她要我扶著她在夜晚走到大街去，然後躺下，我偷偷躲在一棵樹後面，果真看到有人發現了媽媽，也發現她病重，立刻攔下了一部計程車，一開始計程車司機好像不肯載媽媽，看她太髒了吧，說了一堆好話以後，才終於肯去「加里加神廟」，這是德蕾莎修女辦的垂死之家。

◇ entrance（n.）入口處
◇ massive（adj.）巨大的；龐然的
◇ prefer（v.）偏好；偏愛
◇ newspaper and book stand（n.）書報攤
◇ generous（adj.）慷慨的；大方的
◇ establish（v.）成立；創立
◇ lie（v.）躺（註：此動詞的三態變化為 lie – lay – lain）

I was lucky enough to get to beg in front of the Oberoi Grand Hotel, the biggest hotel in Calcutta. The roofed sidewalk in front of the entrance is really wide, and along the street are these massive white pillars. Naturally, the rest of the hotel is white too—it's very beautiful. Even though the hotel guests usually preferred to go in and out by car, there were still quite a few who'd go out for walks because there are newspaper and book stands along the street. When one of them would buy a newspaper, I'd make the most of the opportunity to move in and beg. I found that the Oriental-looking travelers were especially generous. Usually we'd earn about ten rupees (US $0.50) a day. Once, an Oriental traveler gave me fifty rupees.

But my mom left me too. It was three months ago that she got sick. As she grew weaker, I spent all our money trying to buy good food for her to eat, but it was no use. Finally she told me that Mother Teresa had established a Home for the Dying: if someone brought her there, there would be people to take care of her, and she might get better. If she got better, she said, she'd come back to look for me.

She asked me to support her out to the main street, where she lay down. I hid behind a tree to see what would happen. Sure enough, someone found Mom there, saw that she was very sick and called for a taxi immediately. At first, it seemed like the driver refused to let her in his car, probably because she was so dirty. After a great deal of coaxing, however, he finally agreed to take her to the Kalighat Temple—that's where Mother Teresa set up her Home for the Dying.

6-10

◇ immediately (adv.) 立刻地；即時地　　◇ coax (v.) 勸哄；好說歹說
◇ refuse (v.) 拒絕

可是媽媽從來沒有回來，我知道她一定已經去世了。唯一使我感到安慰的是，她去世以前一定有修女們照顧她。

我呢？我感到孤獨極了，除了說，「我沒有爸爸，我沒有媽媽，可憐可憐我吧！」這句話之外，我什麼話都沒有機會說。每天晚上買了一團飯吃，賣飯的人也懶得和我說話。

因為感到孤獨，我和附近的一隻小老鼠變成好朋友，我每天準備一些飯粒餵它，它會來咬我的手，我會索性將它抓起來放在手上親親它，晚上它甚至會和我睡在一起。

忽然，街上來了一大批人，向四周噴藥，那天晚上，小老鼠就不出現了，它到哪裡去了？我無從知道，也很難過。它是唯一的朋友，可是它又不見了。

11-15 第二天，我知道我病了，白天我該到旅館去求乞的，可是我難過得吃不消，中午就回來睡著了。而且我還吐了一次。

下午，來了一些帶口罩的人，他們將我抬上了一輛車子，車子裡大多數好像都是病重的乞丐，我雖然生病，可是因為第一次坐汽車，興

◇ comfort (v.) 安慰；慰藉
◇ lonesome (adj.) 孤獨的；寂寞的
◇ a ball of rice (n.) 飯糰
◇ grain(s) (n.) 穀粒

◇ nibble (v.) (小口地) 吃；(輕輕地) 咬
◇ spray (v.) 噴灑
◇ pesticide (n.) 殺蟲劑
◇ heartbroken (adj.) 傷心的；心碎的

But Mom never came back after that, so I knew she had to be dead. The only thing that comforted me was knowing that there were nuns taking care of her as she died.

And me? I felt so lonesome! About the only thing I ever had a chance to say was "My father is dead, my mother is dead, have pity on me!" Every night, I would buy a ball of rice to eat, but the rice seller never bothered to talk to me.

Because I was lonely, I made friends with a little mouse from the neighborhood. I fed him some grains of rice every night, and when he'd come nibble at my hand, I'd pick him up and kiss him. He even slept with me at night.

Then suddenly one day, a bunch of people came through the street spraying pesticides. That night, the little mouse didn't appear. Where had he gone? I had no way of knowing. I was heartbroken—he had been my only friend, and now he was gone.

The next day, I knew I was sick. I knew I should spend the daylight hours begging by the hotel, but I felt so awful I couldn't stand it, so I went back home to sleep at noon. I even threw up once. **11-15**

That afternoon, some people with masks came and lifted me into a car. It seemed like most of the other people in the car were sick

---

◇ daylight hours (n.) 白天的時間　　　　◇ mask (n.) 口罩
◇ awful (adj.)（指狀況）很糟的；極差的　◇ lift (v.) 抬

奮得不得了，一直對著窗外看，我發現我們已離開了加爾各答，到了鄉下，我想起媽媽告訴我，爸媽過去住在鄉下，真可惜，我們當年如果留著那塊地就好了。

　　我們被送進了一間大房子，有人來替每一位抽了血，有幾位立刻被送走了，大多數都留了下來，我有生第一次有人來替我洗澡、剪指甲、洗頭髮，感到好舒服，可是我被強迫帶上口罩。

　　最令我高興的是我終於走進了有屋頂的房子，睡在一張床上，而且也有人送飯給我吃，可惜我病了，不然這豈不是太好了。

　　令我不懂的是為什麼他們對我這樣好，也不懂為什麼他們不讓我們離開房間，有一次我感到體力還可以，乘門口警衛不在，偷偷溜到走廊上去看屋外的院子，立刻被警衛抓了回來，幾乎要打我，我更不懂的是他們為什麼人人都帶口罩、帶手套，也從不和我們講一句話，我是個小乞丐，沒有問人的習慣，何況我又病了，也沒有力氣問。

◇ thrilled（adj.）很興奮的；很高興的
◇ blood sample（s）（n.）血液採樣
◇ remain（v.）留（下來）

◇ trim（v.）修剪
◇ pampered（adj.）受到呵護寵愛的
◇ （a）gauze mask（n.）棉紗口罩

beggars too. Despite being sick, I was thrilled to be riding in a car for the first time, and I couldn't stop looking out the window. Soon I saw we had left Calcutta and arrived in the countryside. I thought of how Mom had told me that Dad used to live in the country—what a pity it was we didn't still have that piece of land.

They led us inside a big building and drew blood samples from each of us. A few people were immediately taken away, but most remained. For the first time in my life, someone bathed me, trimmed my fingernails and washed my hair—I felt so pampered! But they made me put on a gauze mask.

The thing that made me the happiest was that I finally got to go into a house with a roof and sleep on a bed! Not only that, but people brought me food too. It's too bad I was sick—otherwise it would have been even better.

What I didn't understand was why they were treating me so well, or why they wouldn't let us leave our rooms. Once, when I felt like I had enough energy, I snuck out into the hallway while the security guard wasn't looking so I could see the yard outside, but I got caught right away, and the guard came within an inch of beating me. Another thing I didn't understand was why they all wore masks and gloves and never spoke to me. Being a beggar child, I wasn't in the habit of asking questions, and besides, being sick, I didn't have the energy to ask.

◇ otherwise (adv.) 否則　　　　　◇ security guard (n.) 警衛
◇ treat (v.) 對待　　　　　　　　◇ beat (v.) (毒) 打；(痛) 揍；(海) 扁
◇ energy (n.) 精力；活力；氣力；體力

16-20　　晚上，外面風大雨大，我睡在床上，雖然身體因病而很不舒服，卻有一種無比幸福的感覺，我知道風雨這次淋不到我了。

　　可是我的病越來越重，我不是唯一病重的一位，隔壁的一位已經去世了，有人將他用白布包起來，抬了出去。他們輕手輕腳地做事，就怕打擾了我們。

　　每次醫生來看我的病情，都搖搖頭，我知道我睡去以後，有可能不再醒來。

　　一位修女來了，她來到我的床前，握住我的手，我注意到她沒有帶手套，只帶了口罩，她握我的手時，眼睛裡都是眼淚，她為什麼要哭呢？難道她不知道我已不想再離開這裡了。如果我離開，我要回去做乞丐，而且要做一輩子的乞丐，我沒有一個親人，沒有一個朋友，從來沒有人握過我的手，從來沒有人關懷過我，我為什麼要回去過這種生活？

　　其實，我現在已經心滿意足了，我唯一的願望就是能進入一間有屋頂的房子，睡在一張床上，現在我的願望已經達成了，我真該感激這

◇ howl (v.) 呼號
◇ pour (v.) (指液體)倒；灌；注；湧
◇ torment (v.) 折磨；使……痛苦
◇ indescribable (adj.) 無法形容的

◇ patient (n.) 病人
◇ wrap (v.) 包裹
◇ disturb (v.) 驚擾
◇ shake (v.) 搖

That night, as wind howled and rain poured outside, I slept in my bed. Even though my body was tormented by disease, I had an indescribable feeling of happiness, for I knew the wind and rain wouldn't touch me tonight.

16-20

But I kept getting sicker. I wasn't the only patient in bad shape—the one next door had already passed away. There were people who came and wrapped him in a white cloth and carried him out. They did their work quietly so as not to disturb us.

Every time the doctor came to see how I was doing, he would shake his head. I knew that the next time I fell asleep, I might not wake up again.

Then a nun came in. She walked to the front of my bed and took hold of my hand. I noticed that she wore no gloves—only a mask. As she held my hand, her eyes filled with tears. Why was she crying? Didn't she know that I never wanted to leave this place again? If I left, I'd have to go back to begging, and I'd be a beggar for the rest of my life. I had no family and no friends. No one had ever held my hand; no one had ever cared for me—why would I want to go back to a life like that?

In fact, I'm already content. All I ever wanted was to go inside a house with a roof and sleep on a bed, and now my wish has come true. Oh, how I ought to thank these kindhearted doctors and nurses!

◇ glove(s)(n.)手套
◇ hold(v.)拉；抓；握；抱
◇ content(adj.)知足的
◇ kindhearted(adj.)仁慈的；善良的；好心的

些好心的醫生和護士，我當然有一點好奇，為什麼過去窮人生病都沒有人理，這一次不同了，像我就受到這種舒服的待遇。

21-22　我感到非常的虛弱，在我清醒的時候，我要祈禱，希望爸爸、媽媽、哥哥、姊姊、好心的醫生、護士和修女們，都能夠在來世過得好一些，不要像我這樣一生下來就是叫化子。

不要替我難過，雖然我可能再也不會醒了，可是我現在頭上有屋頂，身下有一張軟軟的床，今天下午有人用不戴手套的手握住了我的手，我還能不滿意嗎？

◇ attract（v.）吸引　　　　　　　　◇ extremely（adv.）極度地；非常地

Of course, I do wonder why I'm being so pampered now when sick poor people never attracted much attention in the past.

I feel extremely weak, but as long as I'm still awake, I pray that my father, mother, brother and sister, as well as these kind doctors, nurses and nuns, will be better off in the next life. I don't want them to be born beggars like me.

21-22

Don't be sad for me. Even though I may not wake up again, at least now I have a roof over my head and a soft bed underneath me, and this afternoon someone held my hand without wearing gloves. What more could I ask for?

◇　(the)next life(n.)來世；下輩子　　　　◇　underneath(prep.)在……下方

（1）文法：補述用法的分詞片語 S＋V＋..., Ving... （2段）

We were both beggars, living in an alley.

我們都是乞丐，住在一條小街上。

解析

讀者可以把原著「我們都是乞丐，住在一條小街上。」分立成兩個句子：「我們都是乞丐。」和「我們住在一條小街上。」寫成英文就是：We were both beggars. We lived in an alley. 但是這兩個句子語意連貫，更重要的是這兩個句子的主詞相同，所以無論中文或英文，都有相同的語法，即是把這兩個句子結合成一個句子，把語意較弱的句子化為分詞片語，放在主要的句子之後，來追加補述這個主要的句子。我們用以下的例子來說明這個過程。

兩個句子：我推開窗戶。我希望能讓月光進來。

I pushed open the window. I hoped to let in the moonlight.

前句為主要語意，予以保留：I pushed open the window.

後句為次要語意，化為分詞片語：hoping to let in the moonlight

前後結合成為（句子＋分詞片語）：I pushed open the window, hoping to let in the moonlight.

小試身手

1. 他睡眼惺忪地下樓來，不知道發生了什麼事。

_____

（2）文法：名詞子句 what S＋V＋... （2段）

If it rained hard, we'd still get wet, but we were lucky to have what we had.

下大雨的時候，我們仍然會被淋溼。可是我們已經是幸運的了。

解析

讀者先要接受「名詞子句就是當作名詞使用的子句」這樣的觀念。在平常閱讀中，名詞常出現在主詞的位置，所以名詞子句也會出現在主詞的位置作句子的主詞。

名詞 theory 作句子的主詞：His theory is correct.

名詞子句 what he has proposed 作句子的主詞：What he has proposed is correct.

名詞也常出現在受詞的位置，所以名詞子句也會出現在受詞的位置作句子的受詞。

名詞 excuse 作句子的受詞：The teacher accepted his excuse.

名詞子句 what he said 作句子的受詞：The teacher accepted what he said.

讀者要留心的是，這個解析重點裡的 what S＋V＋... 只是若干名詞子句裡的一種，在英文文章常看到的往往也是名詞子句，以下提供三例練習。

小試身手

2-1. 她怎麼做到的一直是個謎。

_____

2-2. 我了解時間是太晚了。

_____

2-3. 為何發生這種事讓該地區的居民們都想不通。

_____

（3）習慣用語：have it worse（處境；際遇）更糟糕；更悲慘（2段）

Some kids had it worse—they had no boards to block out the wind and rain.

有的小孩子更可憐，他們沒有木板可以擋掉一部分的風雨。

解析

學習英語碰上習慣用語，千萬要提高警覺。因為習慣用語是日常生活或英語世界文化的產物，對於並非置身於該文化、成長於該環境的英文學習者，自是加倍困難。以這裡的「處境更糟糕」、「際遇更悲慘」來說，再平常不過了，可是要用英文表達何其困難，你會覺得比要求你用英文表達「我前天交了個新朋友」來得更困難。可是當你看到譯文竟然是 had it worse 時，在肅然起敬之餘，你不也有種會心一笑的感覺嗎？

如果我問你：「4321 乘以 1234 除以 8 再開根號等於多少？」你大概會想回答「你把我難倒了。」瞧，這不就是日常生活中的習慣用語嗎？

數學把你難倒了，英文會不會也把你難倒呢？

小試身手

3. 你把我難倒了。

＿＿＿＿＿＿＿＿＿＿＿＿＿＿＿＿＿＿＿＿＿＿＿＿

（4）take cover 遮躲；掩蔽（2段）

Whenever it started to rain, they'd have to search frantically for a place to take cover, and on a bad night, they might not find one where they wouldn't be driven away.

一下雨，就要四處找一個地方躲雨，弄得不好，還會被人趕。

解析

cover 通常作動詞使用，意思是多數人都熟悉的「覆蓋」、「遮蔽」的意思。比如，「他想要隻手遮天。」(He's trying to cover it up.) 在軍事影片裡，大英雄常丟下一句「掩護我」(Cover me.)，然後就英勇向前，去執行九死一生的任務。

在這個重點裡，cover 是個名詞，然而卻仍脫不了「遮護」、「掩蔽」的意思。因而整個片語 take cover 即是「尋求遮蔽」、「得到掩護」之意，常用來表示「想辦法不受到風吹日曬雨淋或不讓任何災禍及身」，和 take shelter (from) 語意相通。

小試身手

4. 在雷雨時躲到大樹下實不足取(不是個很好的想法)。

_____

(5) a string of ... 一連串的(3段)

Dad had been a farmer, but a string of bad harvests made him lose first his ox and then his land.

爸爸是個農人，可是接二連三的壞收成，爸爸先是失去了牛，然後失去了那一塊地。

解析

欲了解這個片語，可以從片語最關鍵的字 string 看起。此字的基本含意為「細線」，所以看到 a string of... 這個片語，可以讓人聯想到如線般「一連串的」或如線般「接連不斷的」。所以譯者用之來詮釋「接二連三」，真是貼切。

> **小試身手**
>
> 5. 我遭逢到困難，不只是一些，而是一大串。
>
> _____

(6) slave away（如奴隸般）做出賣勞力的苦工（3段）

Dad slaved away as a manual laborer until he got sick after I was born and Mom was forced to beg for a living.

爸爸做各種苦工，我生下以後，爸爸病死，媽媽只好求乞為生。

解析

slave 一般作名詞，為「奴隸」之意，但在此處作動詞，作「（如奴隸般）做粗活」解釋。英文中常有「動詞＋ away」的慣用法，如 Fly away.（飛走）；Run away.（跑開）；Fire away.（儘管開槍吧！）

句子中另有 manual laborer 一詞，指的是「粗工」、「勞力工作者」。還有「乞討為生」的英文為 beg for a living，也是讀者可以學習的地方。

> **小試身手**
>
> 6. 他帶著老媽給他的錢到大商場，瘋狂採購。
>
> _____

(7) make the most of the opportunity 善用機會；把握良機（4段）

When one of them would buy a newspaper, I'd make the most of the opportunity to move in and beg.

他們來買報紙，我就趁機上前去求乞。

解析

一般說來，「把握機會」的英文為 take the opportunity，動詞使用 take。這個重點的片語為 make the most of the opportunity，是「充分利用機會」、「把機會利用到極致」的意思。動詞由 take 改為 make，和 the most of... 很有關係。

┌─────────────────────────────────────┐

小試身手

7. 因為我們就快畢業，我們應把握剩餘的時間盡量多多相處。

　　─────────────────────────

└─────────────────────────────────────┘

(8) 文法：關係副詞 where S＋V＋... (6段)

She asked me to support her out to the main street, where she lay down.
她要我扶著她在夜晚走到大街去，然後躺下。

解析

where she lay down 是一個子句（從屬連接詞 where ＋主詞 she ＋動詞 lay down）。其中從屬連接詞 where 本身為關係副詞，因為它之前有一個「先行詞 (the main street)」，因此關係子句 where she lay down 真正的意思為「她躺在大街上」。如果捨關係副詞作連接詞而以對等連接詞取而代之，則以上的句子可以寫成為：She asked me to support her out to the main street, and she lay down (right) there. 反應快的讀者應該很快就領會到 where 和 and... (right) there 兩者間的關係。同時別忘了，除了 where 其他的關係副詞還有三個：when, why 和 how。

┌─────────────────────────────────────┐

小試身手

8-1. 戰爭於1947年爆發，當時該國毫無準備。

　　─────────────────────────

└─────────────────────────────────────┘

8-2. 你可否給我一個你老是上課打瞌睡的理由？

_____

(9) after a great deal of coaxing 好說歹說一番後（6段）

After a great deal of coaxing, however, he finally agreed to take her to the Kalighat Temple—that's where Mother Teresa set up her Home for the Dying.

說了一堆好話以後，才終於肯去「加里加神廟」，這是德蕾莎修女辦的垂死之家。

解析

動詞 coax 為「哄勸」的意思，比方，你已婚的朋友告訴你，小孩真難帶，要說故事哄一番才肯睡覺。這時你就可以客串記者向別人轉播說：My friend says she has to coax her child into sleep by telling stories.

a great deal of coaxing 自然就是「連哄帶騙」；「好說歹說」的意思。

小試身手

9. 妳不覺得用哄勸的有時比用命令來得更有效果？

_____

(10) have pity on... 同情（某人）；憐憫（某人）（8段）

About the only thing I ever had a chance to say was "My father is dead, my mother is dead, have pity on me!"

除了說，「我沒有爸爸，我沒有媽媽，可憐可憐我吧！」這句話之外，我什麼話都沒有機會說。

解析

名詞 pity 相當於中文的「同情心」、「慈悲心」，所以 have pity on someone 自然就是「對某人寄予同情」或「憐憫某人」的意思。英文另有單字 mercy 可以表示「慈悲憐憫」，因此片語 have mercy on... 和 have pity on... 意思和用法大致相同。但前者似乎更常用在情況不利而求饒的時候，比如 Have mercy on me. 就有「放過我」、「饒了我」的意思。

小試身手

10. 父親一直教導我們要憐憫窮困的人。

_____

（11）make friends with... 與（某人）交朋友；結識（某人）（9段）

Because I was lonely, I made friends with a little mouse from the neighborhood.

因為感到孤獨，我和附近的一隻小老鼠變成好朋友。

解析

make friends 是「做朋友」、「交朋友」的意思，是很容易理解的英文。「和某人做（交）朋友」、「結識某人」以 make friends with... 來表達也就理所當然了。

小試身手

11. 他勸我不要和沒有禮貌的人為友。

_____

(12) a bunch of... 一群（10段）

Then suddenly one day, a bunch of people came through the street spraying pesticides.

忽然，街上來了一大批人，向四周噴藥。

解析

a bunch of... 常用來指相當於中文的「一束」、「一捆」、「一紮」。a bunch of flowers「一束鮮花」，把好幾支鉛筆用橡皮筋紮起來成為一捆，可以用 a bunch of pencils 表達。所以再加以引申，聚集成群的人或物也可以用 a bunch of... 來表達。a bunch of wasps 是「一群大黃蜂」而 a bunch of noisy school kids 是「一群吵吵鬧鬧的學童」。

> 小試身手
>
> 12. 不久，一群蚊子在我頭上盤旋。
>
> _____

(13) have no way of knowing 無從知道；不得而知（10段）

Where had he gone? I had no way of knowing.

它到哪裡去了？我無從知道。

解析

把這個句型破解開來，可以發現 have no way 的字面含意為「沒有辦法」，因而 have no way of Ving 也就具備了「沒有（做某事）的辦法」。比如「我沒有辦法計算出來這個工作需要幾個工作天。」英文就要表達為 I have no way of figuring out how many workdays it takes/ would take to complete the task. 這是個很實用的句型，值得學起來。

13. 電池沒電,我無法以行動電話和外界聯繫。

_____

(14) It seems/seemed like... 好像;似乎(12段)

It seemed like most of the other people in the car were sick beggars too.
車子裡大多數好像都是病重的乞丐。

解析

你和某人是多年好友,常在一起聊天,算起來很了解彼此,你知道他很懂得知足惜福,若要以英文表示,可以說 He is content with what he has.

但如果你和某人並不很熟,只是從一些表相或隻字片語而認為某人懂得知足惜福,也許你就可以運用這個句型,在 He is content with what he has. 之前套上一個 It seems like 使之成為 It seems like he is content with what he has. 話說回來,學習英文是一輩子的事業,可不能以現有的成就而自滿。如果把句型裡的動詞改為 look,更是具備「看來好像」的味道。

14. 看來不景氣要持續幾季。

_____

（15） what a pity it is/was 真可惜；真是憾事（12段）

I thought of how Mom had told me that Dad used to live in the country—what a pity it was we didn't still have that piece of land.

我想起媽媽告訴我，爸媽過去住在鄉下，真可惜，我們當年如果留著那塊地就好了。

解析

某人心地善良，經常熱心助人，提到他，大家都說「他真是好人一個！」英文表現起來為 What a nice guy he is! 現在讓我們把「好人一個」改為「憾事一件」，讓句子成為「這真是憾事一件！」一件令人感到遺憾的事或讓當事人覺得惋惜的事，英文用 a (great) pity 表示，所以「這真是憾事一件！」可以寫為 What a (great) pity it is!

小試身手

15. 判斷錯誤讓他投資損失重大。真是遺憾。

_____

（16） for the first time in one's life 一輩子首度；生平第一次（13段）

For the first time in my life, someone bathed me, trimmed my fingernails and washed my hair—I felt so pampered!

我有生第一次有人來替我洗澡、剪指甲、洗頭髮，感到好舒服。

解析

言談裡出現這個片語的機會很高，而且既然 for the first time in one's life 為「生平第一次」，那「某人這輩子第二／三次」當然就可以說成 for the second/third time in one's life 了，而「這輩子最後一次」也就順理成章是 for the last time in one's life 了。

小試身手

16. 我這輩子最後一次把他要的錢滙給他，然後移居國外。

_____

(17) it would have been（even）better 情況會更好（14段）

It's too bad I was sick—otherwise it would have been even better.

可惜我病了，不然這豈不是太好了。

解析

請注意原著「可惜我病了」，這個「我病了」是個過去的事實，所以英譯用 I was sick 來處理。接下來的原著是「不然這豈不是太好了」，這個「這豈不是太好了」並非是過去的事實，因為事實是「狀況並不好」（it was not good）。明明「狀況並不好」，硬要說成「這豈不是太好了」，這就叫作與（過去）事實相反，此時英文就得以假設法來表現：it would have been even better。請讀者用心思考，把 it was not good 和 it would have been even better 做個對比，就會發現，要把和過去事實相反表現出來，就是把表示「過去事實」的動詞（was）更改成為表示「和過去事實相反」的動詞（would have been）。如果表示「和過去事實相反」的動詞是在 if 所引導的子句裡，則寫成（had Vpp）。假設法是我們學習英文的一道難關，的確需要正確的觀念，才能得心應手。以下的練習，不容放過。

小試身手

17-1. 如果昨天晚上他在這裡，我就會把真相告訴他。

_____

17-2. 他沒看到我，否則他會買飲料請我。

_____

（18）come within an inch of Ving... 幾乎要；差點就（15段）

... and the guard came within an inch of beating me.

警衛幾乎要打我。

解析

想做某事（Ving）的欲望已經接近（come）到不足一英吋（within an inch）的距離了，豈不就是中文之內「幾乎就要」或「差點就要」做某事的意思嗎？再舉個例子，你不會游泳，卻不小心落水，就在快作波臣之際，被人救起來，事後回想，真的很幸運，「差點淹死」。這個「差點就淹死」便可以用這個句型來表現：I came within an inch of drowning.

小試身手

18. 他差點被流彈擊中。

_____

（19）文法：分詞構句（15段）

Being a beggar child, I wasn't in the habit of asking questions, and besides, being sick, I didn't have the energy to ask.

我是個小乞丐，沒有問人的習慣，何況我又病了，也沒有力氣問。

解析

上句英譯裡出現兩個分詞構句：being a beggar child 和 being sick。要了解分詞構句，先觀察以下的結構：Ving..., S ＋ V ＋ ... 。所以分詞構句就是這個面貌：Ving...，但是要注意，它的位置在句首，它的動作（Ving）執行者為後面的主詞（S）。用輕鬆有趣的口氣來說，這種結構的主詞比較辛苦歹命，因為它既要執行之後動詞的動作（S ＋ V ＋ ... ）又得執行前面分詞（Ving）的動作，身兼兩職，不辛苦嗎？

以下再舉個實例，幫讀者得到更明晰的概念。

「我放棄了那個計劃。」
I gave up on the plan.

現在把副詞子句「因為知道最好的時機已過」加入上面的句子，使之成為

「因為知道最好的時機已過，我放棄了那個計劃。」
Because I knew the time for it was past, I gave up on the plan.

或「我放棄了那個計劃，因為我知道最好的時機已過。」
I gave up on the plan, because I knew the time for it was past.

以上兩句都可以把 because I knew... 改為 knowing...，使之分別成為
Knowing the time for it was past, I gave up on the plan. 和 I gave up on the plan, knowing the time for it was past. 但是就文法而論，只有在句首位置的 knowing the time for it was past 才以分詞構句名之。讀者看到這裡，要給自己的心得下個結論：分詞構句和副詞子句是一體的兩面，可以把位置在句首的副詞子句精簡為分詞構句，也可以反其道而行，把分詞構句改為副詞子句。

小試身手

19. 在這村子住了二十多年，我很了解它的居民和它的習俗（風土民情）。

　＿＿＿＿＿＿＿＿＿＿＿＿＿＿＿＿＿＿＿＿＿＿＿＿＿＿＿＿

---

(20) have an indescribable feeling of... 對……有一種無法形容的感覺（16段）

Even though my body was tormented by disease, I had an indescribable feeling of happiness, for I knew the wind and rain wouldn't touch me tonight.

雖然身體因病而很不舒服，卻有一種無比幸福的感覺，我知道風雨這次淋不到我了。

解析

可以從 have a feeling of... 這個句型出發，它表示「有種……的感覺」。比如「我有種被遺棄的感覺。」以英文表達起來為 I had a feeling of abandonment.

現在只是把形容詞 indescribable（意思為「無法形容的」、「說不出來的」）植入這個片語，讓它進一步產生了「對……有種說不出來、點滴在心的感覺」這樣的意思。

小試身手

20. 光是在鬼屋近旁就給我一種恐怖的感覺。

_____

---

(21)（be）in bad shape 身體狀況不佳（17段）

I wasn't the only patient in bad shape—the one next door had already passed away.

我不是唯一病重的一位，隔壁的一位已經去世了。

解析

無論是上帝創造的萬物或者是人為設計出來的東西，總有其完好美好的面貌造型，英文為 shape，所以當我們說 in（good）shape 時是表示東西「狀況良好」或者人「身心健康」。反之，當然指的就是東西的「狀況糟糕」、人的「健康不理想」。

小試身手

21. 車輛的狀況很不理想，可是它還是把我們載到要去的地方。

_____

(22) take hold of... 抓；握（19段）

She walked to the front of my bed and took hold of my hand.

她來到我的床前，握住我的手。

解析

take hold of 是個很好、很重要的片語。hold 在此片語裡為名詞，意思為「拿」、「抓」、「握」之意。亦可作動詞，以本句來說，也可以表示為 She took/held my hand in hers.

有過搭乘公車地鐵的經驗吧，上下班尖峰時刻，在擁擠的公車或捷運，你可能只有站著的份，手攀著握環，怎麼說呢？

小試身手

22. 我緊抓握環免得摔倒。

_____

(23) for the rest of one's life 餘生；往後的日子（19段）

If I left, I'd have to go back to begging, and I'd be a beggar for the rest of my life.

如果我離開，我要回去做乞丐，而且要做一輩子的乞丐。

解析

rest 為名詞，在此處為「剩餘」、「殘留」之意，因此 the rest of one's life

指的是在人生某個事件或某個階段後的日子，相當於「餘生」、「往後的日子」，算是很容易學得起來的片語。**to go back to begging**：回去行乞，這裡用 begging 表示行乞的狀態。底下小試身手來嘗試名詞的用法 beggar。

小試身手

23. 他在公司破產後過著如乞丐的生活。

_____

（24）**as long as...** 只要

　　　as well as... 與……一樣（21段）

I feel extremely weak, but as long as I'm still awake, I pray that my father, mother, brother and sister, as well as these kind doctors, nurses and nuns, will be better off in the next life.

我感到非常的虛弱，在我清醒的時候，我要祈禱，希望爸爸、媽媽、哥哥、姊姊、好心的醫生、護士和修女們，都能夠在來世過得好一些。

解析

as long as... 和 as well as... 為兩個外型很近似的片語，但是意義大異其趣。基本上前者常作連接詞，意義相當於中文引導一個表條件的副詞子句「只要」，比如「只要好天氣持續，我們就開放海灘給泳客。」（見「小試身手」）

as well as... 身份比較曖昧，有連接詞的味道，但也看得到有介詞的用法。趨近連接詞用法時，其意義接近中文的「和、與……一樣」，比如「復活節和聖誕節一樣，是個宗教節日。」（見「小試身手」。）

趨近介詞用法時，其意義趨近中文「除了」。比如，「他除了買餐盒給我，還買了張到台東的車票給我。」（見「小試身手」。）

小試身手

24-1. 只要好天氣持續，我們就開放海灘給泳客。

_____

24-2. 復活節和聖誕節一樣，是個宗教節日。

_____

24-3. 他除了買餐盒給我，還買了張到台東的車票給我。

_____

（25）**What more could I ask for?** 夫復何求？還要多強求些什麼呢？（22段）

What more could I ask for?
我還能不滿意嗎？

解析

片語 ask for 為「要求」、「乞求」的意思。「我向媽媽要 800 元買那雙鞋子。」英文表示起來為 I asked my mom for 800 dollars to buy the pair of shoes.「他說他很滿足他所擁有，不想再要求更多東西。」可以寫成 He said he was satisfied with what he had and would ask for nothing more. 如果讀者對以上的解析有所體會，自然就可以聯想到為什麼 What more could I ask for? 是「我還能強求些什麼呢？」。更深入思考，這句話其實是否定的語意，讀者應感覺得到，它真正的意思是「我別無所求。」即 I have nothing more to ask for. 的意思。

小試身手

25. 你給他愈多，他要的也愈多。他不知道適可而止。

_____

 小試身手解答

1. He came downstairs drowsily, not knowing what was going on.

2-1. How she did it has been a mystery.

2-2. I understood that it was too late.

2-3. Why such a thing would happen puzzled the locals.

3. You got me there. 或 Beats me. 或 I have no idea.

4. It is not a good idea to take cover under a big tree in a lightning storm.

5. I encountered difficulties, not just a few, but a string of them.

6. He went to the mall with the money his mom gave him and shopped away.

7. Since we're about to graduate, we should make the most of the time we have left together.

8-1. War broke out in 1947, when the nation was least prepared for it.

8-2. Can you give me a reason why you're always dozing off in class?

9. Don't you think coaxing is sometimes more effective than commanding?

10. Father always taught us to have pity on those in need.

11. He advised me against making friends with rude people.

12. Soon a bunch of mosquitoes were circling over my head.

13. The battery was dead, so I had no way of communicating with the

outside world by mobile phone.

14. It looks like the depression will persist for several more quarters.

15. The misjudgment led to a huge loss of his investment. What a pity.

16. For the last time in my life, I wired him the money he demanded. Then I moved abroad.

17-1. If he had been here last night, I would have told him the truth.

17-2. He didn't see me; otherwise he would have bought me a drink.

18. He came within an inch of being hit by a stray bullet.

19. Having lived in this village for over twenty years, I'm well aware of its people and its customs.

20. Just being near the haunted house gave me an indescribable feeling of terror.

21. The vehicle was in bad shape, but it still took us where we wanted to go.

22. I took hold of a strap in case I stumbled.

23. He lived like a beggar after his company went bankrupt.

24-1. The beach will continue to be open to the swimmers as long as the good weather lasts.

24-2. Easter as well as Christmas is a religious day.

24-3. He bought me a ticket to Taidong as well as a lunch box.

25. The more you give him, the more he asks for. He just doesn't know when to quit.

Newt, Why Did You Kill Me?
紐特，你為什麼殺了我？

1-5　　在小鎮做醫生，和在大城市做醫生，總有點不同，在大城市，大多數醫生只管看病，絕對不過問病人的私事，可是我是科羅拉多州的一個小鎮裡的醫生，難免要管點閒事。

　　前幾天，來了一位癌症末期的病人，四十二歲，白人，男性，父母雙亡，在這個小鎮顯然沒有親人。由他的同事陪他來的，來的時候，病情已經很嚴重，來了以後病情急轉直下，這已是他第三次進醫院，前兩次都是在華盛頓的陸軍醫院治療的，因為他在這裡一家會計公司做事，所以這一次他就來我們這一家小醫院，大概他自己知道這次復發，不可能好了，所以到我們這家小醫院來。他非常合作，雖然有很大的痛苦，卻盡量地不埋怨，好像在默默地忍受他的病痛。

　　他的名字很容易記，是約翰・甘迺迪，和那位被刺的總統完全一樣。

　　約翰在清醒時不太講話，可是睡著以後卻常說夢話，他常叫一個名字「紐特」，有的時候，卻又說「紐特，你為什麼殺了我？」紐特

CD1-6

◇ poke(v.)伸(出；入)；探(出；入)
◇ private affairs 私事
◇ nose-poking 管閒事；刺探打聽閒事
◇ stage(n.)階段
◇ coworker(n.)同事
◇ shape(n.)(指身體健康方面的)狀態

◇ dramatic(adj.)戲劇化的；急遽的
◇ veterans' hospital 退伍軍人醫院
　(註：veteran本意為「老兵」，因此 veterans' hospital 相當於台灣的「榮民醫院」。)

1-5
CD1-5

Being a doctor in a small town is not quite the same as being a doctor in the big city. In the city, most doctors just treat illnesses— they never poke their noses into their patients' private affairs. But as a doctor in a small town in Colorado, I find it hard to avoid having to do a little nose-poking here and there.

A few days ago, we had a patient, a 42-year-old white male, who was in the final stages of cancer. Both his parents were dead, and it was obvious he had no other family in town. When he came in with his coworker, he was already in pretty bad shape, and he soon took a dramatic turn for the worse. This was the third time he had been in a hospital with cancer; the first two times were at a veterans' hospital in Washington. Since he worked at a nearby accounting firm, he had come to us this time. Most likely he knew his cancer wasn't going to get better again, so he just came to our little hospital. In spite of his great pain, he was very cooperative. He seemed to be enduring his suffering in silence, doing his best not to complain.

His name was easy to remember: John Kennedy, same as the assassinated president.

John didn't talk much when he was awake, but he often talked in his sleep. He'd often call out the name Newt, and sometimes he'd go on to say, "Newt, why did you kill me?" The name Newt was a very

---

◇ accounting firm 會計事務所
◇ cooperative (adj.) 合作的；肯配合的

◇ suffering (n.) 痛苦；磨難
◇ assassinate (v.) 暗殺

這個名字很少用,目前眾議院的共和黨領袖的名字叫做紐特,要不是他,我根本不可能認得出這是個名字。

在醫院裡聽到有人在夢裡提到殺人這種詞句,當然不免令人有些緊張,我本來打算不管他的,可是其他同仁們也聽到了。大家都議論紛紛,認為這是件怪事。

6-10　　我們不敢問約翰,看他如此虛弱,不忍去打擾他。因為他的那一位同事每天都來看他,我們決定問他,他的同事說他從來沒有聽過約翰提起叫紐特的人,他同事中也沒有任何一位叫紐特的人。

我發現約翰在越南當過兵,而且有一位當年和他一齊當兵的好朋友,我們找到了他,他也說從未聽過紐特,他對約翰病重感到非常難過,那個週末還特地搭飛機趕來看他。

約翰的病情越來越重,我已發出了病危通知書,通知了那位送他來的同事,他的同事告訴我約翰對他的後事都有安排,遺囑已寫好,交給律師,可是他認為我們仍該弄清楚紐特是誰。

◇ the Republican leader in the House of Representatives 眾議院共和黨領袖(註:the Republican Party 為「共和黨」,所以 the Republican leader 是「共和黨領袖」,至於 the House of Representatives 則指美國國會兩院制度其中之一的「眾議院」,另一院為 the Sanate,中文以「參議院」名之。)
◇ murder(n.)謀殺
◇ originally(adv.)原本;本來

uncommon one—if it weren't for the fact that the Republican leader in the House of Representatives was named Newt, I wouldn't even have recognized it as a name.

In a hospital, it's hard not to feel uneasy when you hear someone talking in his sleep about something like murder. I'd originally intended to ignore it, but some of my colleagues overheard. It wasn't long before everyone was talking about what a strange thing it was.

We didn't want to raise the subject with John—seeing how weak he was, we didn't have the heart to disturb him. Instead, we decided to ask his coworker about it, since he came to see John every day. He said he'd never heard John mention anyone named Newt, and there were no Newts at their firm.

6-10

I did find out that John had fought in Vietnam, though, and he had a buddy who had served with him there. We tracked him down, but he'd never heard of Newt either. He was very sad to hear that John was so ill; he even flew out to see him that weekend.

John's condition continued to deteriorate; it got so bad that I wrote a letter notifying his coworker that he was about to die. John had already made arrangements for his death, his coworker said—he'd written a will and given it to a lawyer. But he still thought we ought to figure out who Newt was.

◇ overhear (v.) 偷聽（偶然聽到別人對話，不是故意的）
◇ raise (v.) 提出
◇ buddy (n.)（感情很要好的）弟兄；哥兒們（註：在此指在軍中服役的同袍。）

◇ track (v.) 追蹤
◇ condition (n.) 狀況
◇ deteriorate (v.) 惡化
◇ notify (v.) 通知
◇ arrangement (n.) 安排（多用複數型）

　　這位同事知道約翰有一本記事本，這次也帶了來，事到如此，也不管隱私權了，我們打開記事本，果真發現了紐特的名字，旁邊有一個電話號碼。電話是芝加哥的，大家公推我打電話。電話接通以後，對方首先報名，「這裡是聖保羅教堂」。我說「我要找紐特」，當時我有點不好意思，因為我連紐特的姓都不知道，好在對方毫不介意，替我接上了紐特，在轉接的時候，我發現紐特是這所教堂的助理牧師。這令我大吃一驚，怎麼扯上了一位牧師？

　　「喂，我是紐特牧師，請問有何貴幹？」說話的人語調非常溫和，他用他的小名，也是一種拉近對方距離的做法，很多神職人員只用他的小名，而故意不提姓。

11-15　　「請問你認不認識約翰・甘迺迪？」

　　「當然認識，他是我的弟弟。他怎麼啦？難道癌症復發了？」

　　於是我告訴他我的身分，也告訴他約翰正病危，既然對方是病人的哥哥，似乎應該來看他。

◇ right to privacy 隱私權
◇ embarrassed（adj.）難為情的；不好意思的
◇ transfer（v.）轉（接）電話
◇ assistant pastor 助理牧師
◇ priest（n.）牧師或神父之類的神職人員

The coworker knew John had an address book, and he brought it with him on his next visit. At this stage of the game, we figured we could justifiably ignore John's right to privacy, so we opened the book. Sure enough, we found Newt's name, and there was a Chicago telephone number beside it. Everyone said I should be the one to make the call. "Saint Paul's Chapel," said the man who answered the phone. "I'd like to speak to Newt," I said. I was a little embarrassed that I didn't know Newt's last name, but luckily he didn't mind; he promptly transferred my call to Newt. As he did so, I found out that Newt was the assistant pastor at the chapel. "What does this have to do with a priest?" I wondered, taken aback.

"Hello, I'm Pastor Newt. What can I do for you?" The speaker's voice was very kind, and he used his first name as a way of lessening the distance between us. A lot of clergymen intentionally avoid mentioning their last names to achieve this effect.

"Do you know a man named John Kennedy?"   11-15

"Of course I know him—he's my younger brother. Is something the matter with him? Don't tell me his cancer's recurred again."

I told him who I was and how John was close to dying. Since he was his brother, I said, he probably ought to come see him.

◇ lessen (v.) 減少
◇ clergyman (n.) 牧師或傳教士之類的神職人員
◇ intentionally (adv.) 有意地；故意地
◇ achieve (v.) 達到；達成
◇ effect (n.) 效果
◇ recur (v.) (指疾病) 復發

　　紐特說他立刻設法搭晚上的飛機來，相信明天一定可以趕到。我卻有一點慌，我告訴他，約翰常在夢裡喊紐特，但又常常說，你為什麼殺了我？紐特聽了我的話，絲毫不表驚訝，他只說他不可能在電話中說明，但明天他就可以有機會解釋清楚。

　　對我來講，這真是一頭霧水，紐特是約翰的哥哥，也是一位說話溫和的牧師，為什麼約翰說紐特殺了他？為什麼紐特也不抗議呢？

16-20　　第二天，紐特趕到了，他和約翰的確有點像，舉止完全是神職人員的樣子，非常謙和。

　　他先問了我約翰的病況，然後邀請我一起進去。

　　約翰正好醒著，看到了紐特高興極了，紐特擁抱了約翰，口中一再地講：「約翰，請原諒我！」

　　以下是紐特的自白：

「我從大學畢業以後，就在一家生化公司做事，由於我的表現非常

◇ panic（n.）驚恐；恐慌
◇ light（n.）說明；解釋；釐清（註：所以 shed some light on 就有如中文的「說清楚」、「講明白」。）
◇ bewildering（adj.）困惑的

◇ soft-spoken（adj.）說話溫文儒雅的
◇ minister（n.）牧師
◇ object（v.）反對
◇ unassuming（adj.）謙和的；不強勢的
◇ embrace（v.）擁抱

Newt said he'd catch a night flight and be here by tomorrow. This threw me into a bit of a panic. I told him that John often called his name in his dreams, but then he'd say, "Why did you kill me?" Newt wasn't surprised in the least. He couldn't explain over the phone, he said, but he'd be able to shed some light on things tomorrow.

All this was utterly bewildering to me. Newt was John's brother and a soft-spoken minister to boot—why would John say he'd killed him? And why hadn't Newt objected?

The following day, Newt arrived. He did look a bit like John. Very unassuming, he looked and acted the part of a clergyman.

16-20

The first thing he did was ask me how John was doing. Then he invited me into John's room with him.

John, who happened to be awake at the time, was overjoyed to see Newt. As they embraced, Newt kept saying, "John, please forgive me!"

This was Newt's confession:
"When I graduated from college, I started working at a biochemical company. Because of my outstanding performance, by 1969 I had been promoted to vice president of our pesticides division. I was

---

◇ confession（n.）坦白；口供
◇ biochemical company 生化公司
◇ outstanding（adj.）傑出的

◇ vice president 組長（president［總裁］以下各部門的負責人皆可稱之。如vice president of marketing［行銷部組長］）
◇ pesticides division 農藥部門

好，一九六九年我已是農藥組的組長，負責製造各種的農藥。

「我們的產品中有一種叫橙劑的農藥，這是一種落葉劑，灑在樹上，葉子就掉了，當然事後還會長回的，在美國中西部，很多農人用這種藥。當時越戰已經打得很厲害。有一天，我忽然想到，如果灑落葉劑到越南的叢林上，可以使躲在叢林裡的北越游擊隊無處逃，因而減低美國士兵的傷亡。

21-25 「於是我寫了一份備忘錄，給了我的上司，兩天以後，我和我的上司就飛到了華盛頓，見到了國防部的一些官員。他們對我的建議極感興趣，也叫我們絕對保密。

「我們公司從此成了國防部的唯一落葉劑供應者，一切保密。我了解人知道秘密總會有麻煩的，也就索性完全不管這件事。

「有一次，有一份公文陰錯陽差地送錯了，不該送給我的卻好端端地放在我的桌子上，我打開一看，發現是有關落葉劑的生產資料，我

◇ agricultural chemical(s)農藥
◇ product(s)(n.)產品
◇ defoliant(n.)落葉劑
◇ spray(v.)噴灑

◇ jungle(s)(n.)叢林
◇ Vietcong guerrilla [gəˋrɪlə](s)越共的游擊隊
◇ casualties(n.)傷亡

responsible for the production of all our agricultural chemicals."

"One of our products was a chemical called Agent Orange. It was a defoliant: if you sprayed it on a tree, its leaves would fall off, although they'd grow back afterward, of course. A lot of farmers used it in the heartland and the West. At that time, the war in Vietnam was in full swing. One day, an idea suddenly occurred to me: if we sprayed defoliants onto the jungles of Vietnam, the Vietcong guerrillas there would be left with nowhere to hide, and American casualties would be reduced.

"So I wrote a memo to my boss about it. Two days later, I flew with him to Washington to see some officials from the Department of Defense. They expressed a strong interest in my idea, which they told us to keep completely secret.

21-25

"After that, our company became the Department of Defense's sole supplier of defoliants. Everything was kept secret. I understood that knowing secrets always gets people into trouble, so I didn't mention the matter again.

"One day, by some strange twist of fate, an official document that I wasn't supposed to see was delivered to me by mistake. Since it was sitting right there in front of me, I opened it to have a look. It turned out to be information on the production of our defoliant. I knew I

◇ memo(n.)備忘錄
◇ the Department of Defense 國防部
◇ supplier(n.)供應商
◇ twist(n.)扭轉；轉變；轉折
◇ document(n.)文件
◇ deliver(v.)傳遞；傳送
◇ production(n.)生產

不該看這種秘密資料的，可是實在忍不住，我一頁一頁地看下去。

「不看則已，一看，我就嚇了一跳，因為我發現賣給國防部的落葉劑，含戴奧辛的成分是普通農藥的一倍。我立刻去見我的上司，告訴他如果使用這種落葉劑，一定會有人因此而產生癌症，包括美軍在內。

「我的上司勸我不要管這種事，他說落葉劑已經在越南使用了，效果極好，軍方大量採購，公司大發利市，股票也因此大為上揚。公司絕對不願意失去這筆生意的。

26-30　「他同時暗示我，軍方不會肯認錯的，如果他們知道我要將事實公布出來，一定會先下手為強，將我暗殺掉，他的話令我毛骨悚然。

「第二天，我收到公司總經理的一封信，信上說公司對我的工作極為滿意，決定給我一筆五十萬元的獎金，我打電話去問我的銀行，他們說的確有一筆五十萬存入了我的戶頭。

◇ classified information 列為機密的消息　　◇ ignore (v.) 置之不管；不予理會
◇ dioxin content 戴奧辛含量　　◇ effective (adj.) 有效的

shouldn't be looking at classified information, but I couldn't help it—
I read on, page after page.

"If I hadn't looked at it, probably nothing would have happened,
but I did look, and what I saw gave me quite a shock. I discovered
that the dioxin content in the defoliant we were selling to the
Department of Defense was twice as high as that of ordinary pesticide.
I immediately went to see my boss and told him that if we used this
defoliant, it would give people cancer, including American soldiers.

"My boss advised me to ignore what I'd read. He said our defoliant
was already being used in Vietnam, it was proving very effective, the
military was buying huge amounts of it, our company was making
a fortune and our stock had gone way up. There was no way the
company was going to let go of this business opportunity.

"At the same time, he hinted that the military wasn't going to
acknowledge they were in the wrong. If they knew I intended to blow
the whistle on them, they would get rid of me before I could. His
words made my hair stand on end.

26-30

"The next day, I received a letter from our general manager. It said
the company was extremely pleased with my job performance and
had decided to reward me with a $50,000 bonus. I called to verify
this with my bank; sure enough, there had been $50,000 deposited
into my account.

◇ acknowledge (v.) 承認　　　　　◇ verify (v.) 證實；確認 (某事的) 真實性
◇ reward (v.) 回饋；酬答　　　　◇ deposit (v.) 存 (款)

「從此，我就被收買了，我的良心雖然有些不安，可是我想反正我又不是在造汽油彈，由於我捨不得這五十萬元，也捨不得這條命，我決定不再張揚這件事。當時我從來沒想到會連累到我的親人。

「你被徵調到越南，我開始緊張起來。

「有一天，你從越南寫信給我，大大誇讚落葉劑，還說如果沒有落葉劑，你恐怕已經陣亡了。這下我知道我罪孽深重，我的主意竟然害到了親弟弟。

31-35　「我立刻辭掉了那份工作。好一陣子，我想自殺，虧得碰到一位老牧師，他勸我以一生的補償來洗淨我的罪。他介紹我到芝加哥的貧民區去做義工，我去了，卻愛上了替窮人服務的工作。後來，一不做，二不休，我念了神學院，成了牧師。

「我一直都在貧民區裡做事，生活也完全變了。過去我是個雅痞型的人，女朋友多得不得了，生活也非常奢侈。現在我下定決心獨身，

◇ conscience(n.)良心；良知
◇ napalm ['nepɑm] bomb(s)油彈；燃燒彈
◇ reluctant(adj.)勉強的；不情願的
◇ haunt(v.)使(某人)苦惱；困擾
◇ draft(v.)徵調(參軍)；徵召(入伍)
◇ action(n.)戰鬥；作戰(片語in action 的意思為「於進行作戰任務中」。)

"I had been bought off. My conscience made me feel a little guilty, but then I figured, 'Hey, at least I'm not making napalm bombs.' Because I was reluctant to part with my five hundred grand, not to mention my life, I decided to keep my mouth shut. At the time, I never imagined that my sin would come back to haunt someone I loved.

"When you were drafted into Vietnam, I started to get nervous.

"One day, you wrote me a letter from Vietnam singing the praises of Agent Orange. You said that without it, you'd probably have been killed in action long ago. That was when I knew how deeply guilty I was—my idea had hurt my own brother.

"I immediately quit my job. For a long time, I wanted to kill myself. Luckily, I met an old priest who urged me to spend the rest of my life making amends for my sin. He gave me an opportunity to go volunteer in a Chicago ghetto. I went, and I fell in love with serving the poor. I liked it so much that I kept on doing it—I went to theology school and became a priest.

31-35

"Since then, I've continued to work in the ghetto, and my life has changed completely. I used to be a total yuppie—I fooled around

◇ urge (v.) 力勸；敦促；強要
◇ ghetto [ˋgɛto] (n.) (特別指少數族裔，尤其是貧困的少數族裔於城市裡集中居住的) 住宅區；貧民窟
◇ theology school 神學校
◇ yuppie (n.) 指年輕多金，注重生活品味而又捨得花錢享受的都市中產階級；雅痞

而且過著非常簡樸的生活。

「你得了癌症，是我意料中的事。因為大批美軍得了癌症，全是因為落葉劑的原因。我一直想將事情真相告訴你，可是一直無法啟口。

「唯一不能了解的，你怎麼知道是我建議使用落葉劑的？」

約翰說這也是偶然，一共有三千多位因落葉劑而患癌症的越戰退伍軍人，大家聯合一致向政府提出告訴。約翰負責調查事情的真相，因此查出了當年向軍方建議的人，就是自己的哥哥。他從此不再管這件打官司的事。他又發現他哥哥變了，由花花公子變成了替窮人服務的牧師，他猜出了原因，他的理智告訴他應該原諒哥哥。

36-40　怪不得約翰只在夢裡會問，「你為什麼殺了我？」可見他雖然理智上原諒他的哥哥，下意識仍對他的哥哥有一些埋怨。

- luxury (n.) 奢侈
- celibate ['sɛləbɪt] (adj.) 獨身的；不婚的
- coincidence (n.) 巧合
- uncover (v.) 揭發
- involvement (n.) 參與
- lawsuit (n.) 官司；訴訟
- transform (v.) 改變；轉變
- compassionate (adj.) 富同情心的；有愛心的

with girlfriends and lived a life of luxury. Now I've resolved to be celibate, and I live very simply.

"I wasn't surprised when you got cancer. Lots of American soldiers got cancer, all because of Agent Orange. I've always wanted to tell you the truth about all this, but I never could figure out how to begin.

"The only thing I don't understand is, how do you know it was me who came up with the idea of using defoliant?"

John said that it had been a coincidence. There were more than three thousand Vietnam veterans who had developed cancer from exposure to defoliants, and they all united to file a class-action lawsuit against the government. John had been responsible for uncovering the truth about Agent Orange. From his research, he learned that the man who had originally given the military the idea was his own brother. After that, he gave up his involvement in the lawsuit. His brother, he discovered, was not the man he had once been—he had transformed himself from a playboy to a compassionate priest. He realized the cause of the change, and his reason told him he should forgive his brother.

No wonder it was only in his dreams that John cried out, "Why did you kill me?" Apparently, although he had forgiven his brother intellectually, he still blamed him subconsciously.

36-40

◇ intellectually（adv.）在知性方面；在理智方面

◇ subconsciously（adv.）在潛意識裡

約翰又說他正打算找他哥哥來，因為他自己知道已經病危了。

紐特一再地承認自己是個懦夫，可是他一再希望我們知道他已改過遷善，而且也已將全部財產捐給了窮人。

就在紐特一再承認自己是懦夫的時候，約翰突然說話了，他說：

「紐特，不要再提懦夫了，我才是一個不折不扣的懦夫。」

我們大家都大為震驚，不懂他的意思。以下是約翰的自白：

41-45　　「我在越南打仗的時候，常要進攻一個村落，因為怕村落裡有游擊隊，我是排長，每次都由我以無線電召來空軍支援，我總是要求空軍投下汽油彈，汽油彈不僅將茅屋燒得一乾二淨，絕大多數的村民也都被活活燒死。

「可是我發現其實村民全是老弱婦孺，從來就沒有發現過任何壯丁的屍體。我應該停止這種使用汽油彈的請求，可是我為了要求安全感，不管有沒有敵人，一概灑下汽油彈。汽油彈發出來的汽油會黏在人的身上，很多人跳到池塘裡去，有的時候，整個池塘都燒起來了。

◇ coward（n.）懦夫；軟弱的人
◇ repent（v.）悔改
◇ donate（v.）捐獻（金錢；血液等）
◇ possession（s）（n.）財產（註：作此意義解釋時常使用複數。）
◇ dumbfounded（adj.）（因為受到驚嚇而）目瞪口呆的；啞然無聲

John then said that he'd been planning on asking his brother to come, since he knew he was about to die.

Again and again, Newt admitted to being a coward, but he really wanted us to know he'd repented—he'd even donated all his possessions to the poor.

As Newt was calling himself a coward, John suddenly spoke. He said:

"Newt, don't mention that word again. I'm the one who's the real coward."

We all stood there dumbfounded, not knowing what he meant. This was John's confession:

"When I was fighting in Vietnam, oftentimes I'd have to attack a village. Because I was afraid there'd be guerillas in the village, as platoon leader, I'd radio for air support every time. I'd always ask the air force to drop napalm bombs, which would not only burn all the grass huts to the ground, but would burn all the villagers alive.

41-45

"But I'd find that the villagers were nothing but women, children, the old and the weak. I never once found the corpse of a young, strong man. I should have stopped asking for napalm. But I always had them drop it, no matter whether there were enemies there or not, because it made me feel safer. The napalm from the bombs would stick to people's bodies: lots of them would jump into ponds after they caught fire, and sometimes the whole pond would start burning.

◇ platoon [plə`tun] leader（指軍隊編制中　◇ corpse（n.）屍體
　的）排長

「我也曾親眼看到一個母親在臨死以前還抱著她的孩子，孩子已死了，母親仍在燃燒之中，雖然如此，她還是緊緊抱著她的孩子。

「戰事結束了，這種汽油彈將人活活燒死的回憶，卻永遠跟隨著我，我決定永遠不結婚，因為我覺得我殺了這麼多無辜的人，沒有資格享受天倫之樂了。

「如果說誰是懦夫，我才是懦夫，而且我才是罪惡深重的人。」

約翰很吃力地講了這番話，一種令人不安的安靜降臨到病房。好一陣子，我們誰都說不出話來。幾分鐘以後，還是約翰打破了沉默，「紐特，你是牧師，由你替我做臨終祈禱吧！」紐特以眼光問我的意見，我點點頭，以我的經驗，任何人說出這種懺悔的話以後，不久以後就要離開我們了。

46-48　　當天下午，約翰平安地離開了。紐特一直陪著他。我們兩人眼看著儀器上所顯示的心跳完全停止。他謝謝我，但感慨萬千地向我說，「醫生，我和我弟弟從來不曾想過要殺過任何人，我們也都曾想過做醫生，專門做救人的工作。」

◇ cling（v.）緊緊依附（註：在此處作「緊緊抱住」解釋。）
◇ unworthy（adj.）不配的；不值得的
◇ labored（adj.）辛苦的；費勁的

"Once I saw a mother holding her child just before she died. It was already dead, and she was burning, but she still clung tightly to it.

"The war may have ended, but the memory of those napalm bombs burning people to death stayed with me. I decided not to get married—after killing so many innocent people, I considered myself unworthy to enjoy the happiness of having a family.

"If you want to talk about who's a coward, I'm the coward. And I'm the one who's guilty of the greater sin."

After John finished his labored confession, an uneasy quiet descended on the room. For a long time, none of us could speak. A few minutes later, it was John once again who broke the silence: "Newt, you're a priest. Would you pray for me before I die?" Newt asked me with his eyes what I thought. I nodded—in my experience, anyone who made that kind of confession would leave us soon afterward.

That afternoon, John passed away peacefully, with Newt still at his side. The two of us watched as the heartbeat displayed on the monitor stopped completely. He thanked me, but said to me with tremendous remorse, "Doctor, my brother and I never wanted to kill anyone. Both of us used to aspire to be doctors so we could help people for a living."

46-48

◇ descend (v.) 降下；下降
◇ heartbeat (n.) 心跳
◇ tremendous (adj.) 龐大的；極大的
◇ remorse (n.) 悔恨自責；良心譴責
◇ aspire (v.) 立志要……；嚮往要……

　　當天，當我回家的時候，我感到好冷。過去我總以為戰爭最大的恐怖是戰爭中這麼多無辜的人被殺，今天我才知道戰爭最大的恐怖，是將善良的人變成了劊子手。

◇ chilled（adj.）寒冷的　　　　　　　　◇ innocent（adj.）無辜的

When I got home that day, I felt chilled to the bone. I used to think that the most horrible thing about war was how it takes the lives of so many innocent people. Only today did I realize that actually, the most horrible thing about war is how it turns good people into murderers.

◇ murderer (n.) 殺人兇手

(1) poke one's nose into... 干涉；管閒事（1段）

In the city, most doctors just treat illnesses—they never poke their noses into their patients' private affairs.

在大城市，大多數醫生只管看病，絕對不過問病人的私事。

解析

你喜歡別人把鼻子（one's nose）「伸」（poke）「入」（into）到你的私人領域或個人事務嗎？應該沒有人吧。所以英文用 poke one's nose into... 這個成語來表示「干涉」或「管閒事」，實在傳神之至。

小試身手

1. 他真是好管閒事的傢伙。他總是四處打探他不應該知道的事情。

_____

---

(2) find it hard to V 要……也難；難以不（1段）

But as a doctor in a small town in Colorado, I find it hard to avoid having to do a little nose-poking here and there.

可是我是科羅拉多州的一個小鎮裡的醫生，難免要管點閒事。

解析

在看完英譯後，讀者大概會有一種感覺，someone finds it hard 和 it is difficult 兩者原來相差無幾，基本上都在表示「某事做來困難」。這兩個片語通常用在比較普遍一般的情況（非個人特別經驗）或是用在過去的事件中（參考本題的小試身手）。例如：She finds it hard to breathe while swimming. 或 It is difficult for her to breathe while swimming.

小試身手

2. 要我忘了她也難。

_____

(3) in the final stage（of）（某種疾病）末期（2段）

A few days ago, we had a patient, a 42-year-old white male, who was in the final stages of cancer.

前幾天，來了一位癌症末期的病人，四十二歲，白人，男性。

解析

這個片語不僅用於病情，它也可以指任何過程的最後階段。比如：「沒人能夠理解該計劃何以在最後階段喊停。」英文表示起來為：No one could figure out why they called the project to a halt when it reached its final stage.

小試身手

3. 這棟建築已快完工了。

_____

(4) take a（dramatic）turn for the worse 轉變得更差（更糟）（2段）

When he came in with his coworker, he was already in pretty bad shape, and he soon took a dramatic turn for the worse.

由他的同事陪他來的，來的時候，病情已經很嚴重，來了以後病情急轉直下。

解析

(a)turn 在這個成語裡是名詞，作「轉彎」、「轉變」解釋。轉彎可以向左轉，

向右轉。轉變可以變好，也可能變差。此處 take a turn for the worse 當然指的是從已經不是很好而「變得更差了」。現在又加上形容詞 dramatic，它的本意是「戲劇性（化）的」，帶有「大幅度的」、「急遽的」之意。如果用 abrupt 或 sharp 兩字來取代 dramatic 也可以達到同樣的效果。

小試身手

4.　那個國家殘破的經濟局勢因為戰爭而更加惡化。

_____

（5）if it were not for the fact that... 要不是（4段）

The name Newt was a very uncommon one—if it weren't for the fact that the Republican leader in the House of Representatives was named Newt, I wouldn't even have recognized it as a name.

紐特這個名字很少用，目前眾議院的共和黨領袖的名字叫做紐特，要不是他，我根本不可能認得出這是個名字。

解析

細心的讀者會發現，本系列從第一輯到目前您所閱讀的第四輯，只要是和假設語氣觀念有關，總會花一些篇幅解說。此處也是，if it were not for the fact that... 原意是「如果不是因為（有）這個事實」或「要不是有這個事實」，也就是原來就有這個事實存在，說話者做了個反向思考，假想沒有這個事實存在。就英文而言，必須以假設語氣表示，而關鍵就在假設法動詞（此處為 were）。以上是就理論理，以下用實例說明。

事實：It is a fact that my parents are old. I won't study abroad.

現在根據以上做和事實相反的假想，結果為：要不是我父母年紀老邁的事實，我就出國讀書去。

假想：If it weren't for the fact that my parents are old, I would study abroad.

對比上下兩句，讀者應觀察得到此處從事實到假想，其間動詞的變化，即：

it IS a fact that... → If it WERE not for the fact that...

I WON'T study... → I WOULD study...

小試身手

5. 要不是因為大貓熊數量減少，我們不會知道人類文明對牠們的生存威脅有多大。

_____

（6）it isn't/wasn't long before... 很快；過沒多久（5段）

It wasn't long before everyone was talking about what a strange thing it was.

大家都議論紛紛，認為這是件怪事。

解析

眼尖的讀者會發現，it wasn't long before 在中文原著裡並沒有可資對應的字詞。我自己推想，譯者採取了「意譯」的翻譯策略，也就是根據原著的精神，適時添上這個 it wasn't long before，讓譯文更加通暢。就這故事來說，在事情發生之後，「大家隨即在言談中認為這真是怪事一件」，這個「隨即談到」就把原著「議論紛紛」的精神傳達出來。

小試身手

6. 他很快（隨即）又站起來發表那個聲明。

_____

(7)　raise the subject with... 和（某人）談論及某事（6段）

do not have the heart to... 沒那個心腸；不忍心

We didn't want to raise the subject with John—seeing how weak he was, we didn't have the heart to disturb him.

我們不敢問約翰，看他如此虛弱，不忍去打擾他。

解析

第一個片語的核心字眼為 subject，意義為「話題」、「議題」，所以整個片語的基本含意為「提出 (raise)」「話題 (the subject)」「和 (with)」某人討論，也就是「和某人言及某事」或「就教某人某事」。第二個片語的核心字眼為 heart，基本含意為「心」，可以指具體的「心臟」，亦可指抽象的「心情」，heart 同時帶有「勇氣」之意。因此整個就是「不忍心」或「沒那個勇氣」。

小試身手

7-1. 當我跟他提這話題時，他很不高興。

7-2. 我就是不忍心告訴她她的狀況不好。

---

(8)　track someone down 找到某人（7段）

We tracked him down, but he'd never heard of Newt either.

我們找到了他，他也說從未聽過紐特。

解析

track someone down 指的是千辛萬苦，用盡方法，把某人的下落找到或者尋到某人。過程就像獵人，藉著辨認獵物的足印蹤跡 (track)，窮追不捨，最後終於擒獲獵物。

8. 可靠來源（所提供）的線報協助警方很快追捕到嫌犯。

_____

(9) make arrangements for... 安排（某事）；為（某事）預作安排（8段）

John had already made arrangements for his death, his coworker said—he'd written a will and given it to a lawyer.

他的同事告訴我約翰對他的後事都有安排，遺囑已寫好，交給律師。

解析

這個片語很實用，而且很好學。「做安排」當然就是 make arrangements，舉例來說，「我已經做了必要的安排。」英文為：I have made all necessary arrangements.

至於是為什麼事情做安排，則添個介詞 for，其後再接那件事情就可以了。

9. 台北正在為今年十月在此間舉行的國際會議做準備。

_____

(10) justifiably 理直氣壯地；合情合理地（9段）

At this stage of the game, we figured we could justifiably ignore John's right to privacy, so we opened the book.

事到如此，也不管隱私權了，我們打開記事本。

解析

把它提出來當重點看，因為它是個不太好理解、不太好使用的字。單看這個

字，很不容易確定它的意思，如果把它放在句子裡，在前後文的襯托下，它的意思就比較清楚的浮現出來，比方說在上句英譯中，這個就很趨近中文「理直氣壯地」、「算是合情合理的」、「沒什麼不對」、「可以交代得過去」這方面的意思。因此原著和英譯所透露的訊息是，即使打開記事本是無視他人的隱私權、是不對的、不應為的，只是事已至此，也管不了那麼多了，「不理會約翰的隱私權 (ignore John's right to privacy)」一事，也「將就說得過去 (justifiably)」了。

另外，justifiably 是副詞，動詞為 justify，有句很有名的話說「為達目的不擇手段。」英文為：The end justifies the means. 言下之意，目的 (end) 可以把手段 (means) 合理化 (justify)。這樣的話有無道理，就看讀者個人的自由心證了。

小試身手

10. 甲：我可以摘越過圍籬長到我院子來的蘋果嗎？

　　_____

　　乙：我認為沒什麼不可以。

　　_____

---

(11) (be)taken aback 大吃一驚；嚇一大跳（9段）

"What does this have to do with a priest?" I wondered, taken aback.
這令我大吃一驚，怎麼扯上了一位牧師？

解析

(be)taken aback 作「大吃一驚」、「嚇一大跳」著實令人費解，需要用一點強記的工夫。但是仔細想想，當你聽到某個消息，看到某種意想不到的場面，你是不是整個人會為之一震，程度再強一點，還可能順勢往後倒退一步甚至傾倒 (aback)，所以 (be)taken aback 用來表示受到突然的驚嚇不也很

自然？

小試身手

11. 當我揭發他的密謀時，他顯然非常驚愕。

_____

---

(12) throw someone into a panic 令某人驚慌（14段）

This threw me into a bit of a panic.

我卻有一點慌。

解析

整個片語的核心字眼為 panic「恐慌」、「驚恐」，所以 throw someone into a panic 指的是「使某人陷入恐慌」。英譯中另外在之前又加了一個片語 a bit of，其意思是「有點」、「些微」，因而 threw me into a bit of a panic 就有了「令我有點驚慌」的意思。恐慌的經驗大家都有過，可是你可否曾經恐慌到手腳麻痺，不聽使喚的程度呢？

小試身手

12. 我恐慌到人都快癱了。

_____

---

(13) shed（some）light on things 把事情說清楚講明白（14段）

He couldn't explain over the phone, he said, but he'd be able to shed some light on things tomorrow.

他說他不可能在電話中說明，但明天他就可以有機會解釋清楚。

解析

就物理學來說，人的眼睛看得到東西倒不一定是眼睛厲害，而是物體反射了光線。在一個黑暗不見天日的密室裡，眼睛再亮，也看不到什麼。可是如果你手上有把手電筒，把光 (light) 投射 (shed) 在桌椅之類的東西物體 (things) 上 (on)，讓這些物體將光反射，眼睛就看到這些東西了。所以 shed(some)light on things 指的是「把事情弄清楚」。

小試身手

13. 那位警探／偵探的調查讓案件更加清楚。

_____

(14) act the part of... 舉手投足全為……的樣子（16段）

Very unassuming, he looked and acted the part of a clergyman.

他舉止完全是神職人員的樣子，非常謙和。

解析

不妨把 the part of... 想像成「的角色」，所以 the part of a clergyman 不就是「神職人員的角色」嗎？動詞 look 指的是「（外表）看起來」而 act 則指「表演」或「演戲」，那麼 look and act the part of a clergyman 不就傳達了「外表看起來像神職人員，而且神職人員的角色也演得絲絲入扣」的意思？

小試身手

14. 他成功擔任救援投手，幫助球隊贏得首勝。

_____

（15）in full swing 全面展開（20段）

At that time, the war in Vietnam was in full swing.

當時越戰已經打得很厲害。

解析

鐘擺由左而右，再由右而左的運動，英文用 swing 這個字來詮釋。擺幅可以很小，也可能很大，而既然是 in full swing，那就表示擺幅已經大到不能再大。因此，片語 in full swing 就可以用來表示某事的發展已經全面展開，就像中文所謂的「正逢其盛」、「如火如荼」。

小試身手

15. 反戰運動在六○年代正逢其盛。

_____

（16）an idea suddenly occurred to someone 某人突然想到（20段）

One day, an idea suddenly occurred to me...

有一天，我忽然想到……

解析

中文為母語的人思考模式為「我忽然想到」，所以習慣上會以「我（I）」為主詞，很想把句子寫成：I think...。現在發現英文竟然是 An idea occurs/ occurred to me...，一時真的很難適應。其實中文和英文在這一點的表現手法真的差異很大。occur to 是個既定特殊用法，後面一定要加想到這念頭的「人」，念頭絕對是「人」想出來的，所以句型即為 occur to someone。

學習外語，就怕碰到這一類東西，因為它令人一時適應不來，但多看它一眼，多思考它幾回，也就習慣了。

小試身手

16. 我突然想起我有個大學好友住在這小鎮。

_____

（17）by some strange twist of fate 陰錯陽差（23段）

One day, by some strange twist of fate, an official document that I wasn't supposed to see was delivered to me by mistake.

有一次，有一份公文陰錯陽差地送錯了，不該送給我的卻好端端地放在我的桌子上。

解析

譯者使用 by some strange twist of fate 來詮釋「陰錯陽差」，真是神來之筆，令人為之拍案叫絕。

人生呀！命運呀！大概只有極少數人的人生是扶搖直上，平順稱心。多數人一生起起伏伏，有的人甚至命途坎坷。人的一生，人的命運 (fate) 多的是彎來繞去，轉來扭去 (twist) 的時候。有的人不向命運屈服，向命運挑戰，終得柳暗花明。有的人卻被命運無情地擊倒在地，爬不起來。上天也許不盡公平，命運也許不盡平直，但要人生無憾，總要有「不認命」的精神。

小試身手

17. 我的座位陰錯陽差地被安排在哈利波特座位旁邊。

_____

（18）give someone（quite）a shock 嚇了某人一跳（24段）

If I hadn't looked at it, probably nothing would have happened, but I did look, and what I saw gave me quite a shock.

不看則已，一看，我就嚇了一跳。

解析

這個片語不難理解，應該可以手到擒來。甚至可以順藤摸瓜，找到幾個相似的東西來學。比方，桌上成堆的書「讓我頭痛不已」。還有，看到打破的窗戶「我心臟病都快發作了」。請到以下的小試身手練習這兩句。

小試身手

18-1. 桌上成堆的書讓我頭痛不已。

_____

18-2. 看到打破的窗戶我心臟病都快發作了。

_____

（19）twice as high/much/many as... 兩倍之（高，多）（24段）

I discovered that the dioxin content in the defoliant we were selling to the Department of Defense was twice as high as that of ordinary pesticide.

我發現賣給國防部的落葉劑，含戴奧辛的成分是普通農藥的一倍。

解析

先看以下這兩句：

（一）「我姊姊賺的錢是我的兩倍。」My sister earns twice as much as I do.

（二）「她的朋友比我的多兩倍。」She has three times as many friends as me（或 as I do）.

對於倍數的說法有點概念了嗎？

小試身手

19-1. 這本書是你手上那本的兩倍厚。

_____

19-2. 這塊金屬是那塊的五倍重。

_____

(20)　make a fortune 大發利市；大賺其錢（25段）

　　　go way up（價格）大漲；上揚

...our company was making a fortune and our stock had gone way up.
……公司大發利市，股票也因此大為上揚。

解析

英文用 a fortune 指「一大筆錢」。有人看到你駕的愛車，身上的名牌，迭聲讚美，這時你可以酷酷地說：「這些東西花了我不少錢。」（見小試身手 20-1）

go up 本來就是「上升」、「上漲」、「上揚」的意思，在中間加入一個 way，變成 go way up，更表示上漲的幅度很大，有一路飆升的味道。買賣股票的人都有股價忽上忽下、如洗三溫暖的感覺。無論你是股市投資客與否，都可以到小試身手 20-2 來體驗一下滋味。

20-1. 這些東西花了我不少錢。

_____

20-2. 我的股票在下跌之前大漲了好幾天。

_____

（21）blow the whistle on someone 揭穿（某人）；揭發（某人）（26段）

If they knew I intended to blow the whistle on them, they would get rid of me before I could.

如果他們知道我要將事實公布出來，一定會先下手為強，將我暗殺掉。

解析

blow the whistle 就字面看為「吹口哨」之意。這裡指「吹口哨示警。」blow the whistle on someone 指的是「吹哨示意某人有問題」，有「告發或揭穿某人」的意思，特別常用在揭發公司不法犯罪情境。

英譯裡另有 would get rid of me 一語，表示「把我幹掉」、「將我除去」，這樣的用法，值得注意。

21. 因為揭發了公司非法的行銷手法，她變得有名了。

_____

（22）make my hair stand on end 毛骨悚然；不寒而慄（26段）

His words made my hair stand on end.
他的話令我毛骨悚然。

解析

中文有「令某人寒毛直豎」的說法，用 make my hair stand on end 來詮釋最貼切不過了。平常人的頭髮伏貼在頭皮上，情緒激動時才會怒髮衝冠或寒毛倒豎。stand on end 為「（倒）立起」之意，所以 make my hair stand on end 就是「讓某人頭（毛）髮都（倒）立起來」，其驚悚恐怖的感覺可以想見。

小試身手

22. 對於吸血鬼如何處置受害者的描述讓我寒毛直豎。

_____

（23）be bought off 被收買（28段）

I had been bought off. My conscience made me feel a little guilty, but then I figured, 'Hey, at least I'm not making napalm bombs.'
我就被收買了，我的良心雖然有些不安，可是我想反正我又不是在造汽油彈。

解析

be bought off 為 buy someone off 的被動語態。當人被物化的時候，或者當某人把錢看得比名譽或誠信更重要時，這個人是很有可能被金錢收買的，很可悲吧。

23. 他是個正直的人。你不可能收買他。

_____

(24) part with... 割捨；放棄（28段）

Because I was reluctant to part with my five hundred grand, not to mention my life, I decided to keep my mouth shut.
由於我捨不得這五十萬元，也捨不得這條命，我決定不再張揚這件事。

解析

從字面看，片語 part with... 的意思是「和分開」，也就是「不要某個東西」或「捨棄了某個東西」的意思。另外英譯用 five hundred grand 來表示「五十萬元」。口語英文用 grand 指美金一千元，所以 five hundred grand 就是美金五十萬元。另一個口語為 keep one's mouth shut，字面上的意思為「閉緊嘴巴」，也是「緊守口風，不能說出去」的意思。

24. 這個項鍊是她送的禮物。出再多的錢我也不會割愛。

_____

(25) come back to haunt someone 報應；回過頭來侵擾某人（28段）

At the time, I never imagined that my sin would come back to haunt someone I loved.
當時我從來沒想到會連累到我的親人。

[解析]

haunt someone 指的是鬼魅幽魂「纏擾某人不放」，因此 come back to haunt someone 就很接近中文的「輪迴報應在某人身上」。

[小試身手]

25. 今世所造的業會在來世得到報應。

_____

(26) sing the praises of... 稱頌；讚揚（30段）

One day, you wrote me a letter from Vietnam singing the praises of Agent Orange.

有一天，你從越南寫信給我，大大誇讚落葉劑。

[解析]

中文有「歌頌」一詞，用以表示對某人或某事至為推崇。真沒料到，英文竟然也有這麼近似的表達法 sing the praises of...，德業事功之高，到了讚美之詞（the praises）都可以歌之詠之（sing），應該很令人折服吧。

英譯中另有 Agent Orange 一語，指的是越戰時使用的落葉劑（defoliant），又名「橙劑」。

[小試身手]

26. 他相信高科技的價值。你可以聽到他歌頌高科技。

_____

(27) make amends for one's sin 彌補罪愆；補過贖罪（31段）

Luckily, I met an old priest who urged me to spend the rest of my life making amends for my sin.

虧得碰到一位老牧師，他勸我以一生的補償來洗淨我的罪。

解析

make amends 為「彌補」、「修補」之意，因此片語 make amends for one's sin 當然表示「彌補某人之過」。sin 為「罪過」之意，指的是牴觸良心道德或宗教戒律的過失，而非法律層面上的「犯罪」。

小試身手

27. 我很抱歉。我不知道我如何能夠彌補我對你的名譽所造成的損害。

_____

(28) fool around with... 和……廝混（32段）

I used to be a total yuppie—I fooled around with girlfriends and lived a life of luxury.

過去我是個雅痞型的人，女朋友多得不得了，生活也非常奢侈。

解析

譯文裡 fooled around with girlfriends 大約就是「和女朋友們玩玩」，到處鬼混；也有可能暗指複雜的性關係。要謹慎使用。

a life of luxury 指的是「奢侈的生活」，而 live a life of luxury 指的是「過著奢侈的生活」。

28. 當大多數和他同年紀的年輕人正在努力以求事業有成時，他和酒肉朋友到處鬼混。

_____

(29) come up with the idea of... 提出（某）構想；想到（某）辦法（34段）

The only thing I don't understand is, how do you know it was me who came up with the idea of using defoliant?

唯一不能了解的，你怎麼知道是我建議使用落葉劑的？

解析

come up with 為「提出」、「想到」之意，因此 come up with the idea of... 為「想出構想」、「想到辦法」的意思。

29. 他答應接受我提出的任何構想。

_____

(30) develop（a certain disease）from exposure to... 因接觸而染（某）病（35段）

There were more than three thousand Vietnam veterans who had developed cancer from exposure to defoliants, and they all united to file a class-action lawsuit against the government.

一共有三千多位因落葉劑而患癌症的越戰退伍軍人，大家聯合一致向政府提出告訴。

解析

核心字眼為 exposure 為「接觸」，但這種接觸是指讓人或物受到風吹日曬雨淋或其他物質等。比如「接觸到過量的輻射很危險。」以英文表示為：Excessive exposure to radiation is dangerous.

在英譯中 had developed cancer 為「得癌症」，而 from exposure to defoliants 則是「因為沾到落葉劑」之意，因而 had developed cancer from exposure to defoliants 為「因為沾到落葉劑而得癌症」的意思。

小試身手

30. 即使曝曬在陽光下一下子是健康的，過量曝曬則會引發皮膚癌。

_____

（31）not the man he had once been 不是昔日的他；變了個人
　　　（35段）

His brother, he discovered, was not the man he had once been—he had transformed himself from a playboy to a compassionate priest.
他又發現他哥哥變了，由花花公子變成了替窮人服務的牧師。

解析

He's not what he was. 這句話有兩層不同的意思。往好的方向講，就是由差變好，「他已非吳下阿蒙。」往壞的方向說，就是由好變差，「他變壞了，不是以前的他了。」英譯 his brother was not the man he had once been 與 he is not what he was 是一樣的意義。前句要寫成 his brother was not what he had once been，後句要寫成 he is not the man he was，都是可以的。區別在前句用的是過去式（was）和過去完成式（had once been），後句用現在式（is）和過去式（was）。

從接續在後的句子 he had transformed himself from a playboy to a compassionate priest「由花花公子變成了替窮人服務的牧師」，我們可以知道，此處「他哥哥變了」（his brother was not the man he had once been）指的是「改過遷善，重新做人」。

小試身手

31. 請原諒我——我已不再是過去的我。

＿＿＿＿＿＿＿＿＿＿＿＿＿＿＿＿＿＿＿＿

（32）admit to Ving... 坦言或招認（做了某事）（38段）

Again and again, Newt admitted to being a coward, but he really wanted us to know he'd repented—he'd even donated all his possessions to the poor.

紐特一再地承認自己是個懦夫，可是他一再希望我們知道他已改過遷善，而且也已將全部財產捐給了窮人。

解析

片語 admit to Ving... 相當於中文的「供出（某事實）」，「坦言（有某情事）」。中文諺語云：「人非聖賢，熟能無過。」西洋諺語也有如下的話：To err is human.

只要不蓄意犯錯，都是可以原諒的。重點在能知過改過，是不是呢？

小試身手

32. 他坦言使用過（禁）藥兩三次而且深表悔意。

＿＿＿＿＿＿＿＿＿＿＿＿＿＿＿＿＿＿＿＿

(33) burn someone alive 活活燒死（40段）

I'd always ask the air force to drop napalm bombs, which would not only burn all the grass huts to the ground, but would burn all the villagers alive.

我總是要求空軍投下汽油彈，汽油彈不僅將茅屋燒得一乾二淨，絕大多數的村民也都被活活燒死。

解析

學習這個重點，當然要注意形容詞 alive 的用法。其他類似的例子有「活埋」、「活捉」、「生吃／活活吃掉」。有興趣試試身手嗎？難度較高，請小心以對。

小試身手

33-1. 昆蟲被蜥蜴活生生吃掉。

_____

33-2. 好幾百名受傷的俘虜遭到活埋。

_____

33-3. 要活捉逃犯。

_____

---

(34) no matter whether... 無論有否（41段）

But I always had them drop it, no matter whether there were enemies there or not, because it made me feel safer.

可是我為了要求安全感，不管有沒有敵人，一概灑下汽油彈。

解析

我們常常在閱讀中碰到 no matter，姑且就直接把它視為「無論」，後面常跟著一些疑問詞，常見的有 no matter when...（無論何時），no matter where...（無論何處），no matter how...（無論如何），no matter who...（無論誰），no matter what...（無論什麼），no matter which...（無論哪一個）。後面這兩個比較少見 no matter whether... 和 no matter why... ，但它們還是存在的。在以上的英譯裡就出現了，整個 no matter whether there were enemies there or not 是個副詞子句，修飾主要子句（I always had them drop it）的動詞 had(them drop it)。

表示在「有敵人也好，沒有敵人也好」的情況下，都要求「投彈」。有此可見當時越戰已經打到多麼瘋狂不理性的地步了。

小試身手

34. 我數學再怎麼用功，總拿到不及格的成績。

＿＿＿＿＿＿＿＿＿＿＿＿＿＿＿＿＿＿＿＿＿＿＿＿＿＿＿＿＿＿＿＿＿＿＿＿

（35）stick to... 黏貼；緊緊附著（42段）

The napalm from the bombs would stick to people's bodies: lots of them would jump into ponds after they caught fire, and sometimes the whole pond would start burning.

汽油彈發出來的汽油會黏在人的身上，很多人跳到池塘裡去，有的時候，整個池塘都燒起來了。

解析

stick 是動詞，後面常隨著介詞 to，整個片語的意思為「黏住」、「緊貼著」。要注意 stick 是不規則動詞，其過去式為 stuck，過去分詞也是 stuck；另外，sticky 是形容詞，意思為「黏的」、「有黏性的」。

小試身手

35-1. 我不小心讓口香糖黏到頭髮了。

_____

35-2. 膠帶摸起來黏黏的。

_____

（36）cling to 緊抱不放；緊摟（43段）

It（her child）was already dead, and she was burning, but she still clung tightly to it

孩子已死了，母親仍在燃燒之中，雖然如此，她還是緊緊抱著她的孩子。

解析

上個重點裡的動詞 stick 著重在「黏」、「緊緊附著」；這個重點裡的動詞 cling 則具有「緊靠」、「緊抱住」，後面一般也隨著介詞 to 以表示緊抱的對象。

小試身手

36. 我緊緊抱住樹幹隨波逐流，直到獲救。

_____

（37）consider oneself unworthy to V 自覺不配（44段）

I decided not to get married—after killing so many innocent people, I considered myself unworthy to enjoy the happiness of having a family.

我決定永遠不結婚，因為我覺得我殺了這麼多無辜的人，沒有資格享受天倫之樂了。

解析

形容詞 unworthy 為「不配」、「不夠格」之意，因此 consider oneself unworthy to V 就表示「自認為不配做某事」。

小試身手

37. 我自覺不配再(繼續)擔任那個職務。

_____

(38) be guilty of... 犯……之罪 (45段)

And I'm the one who's guilty of the greater sin.
而且我才是罪惡深重的人。

解析

be guilty of... 是常用而重要的片語，其基本含意為「犯……之罪」。另有因犯錯而「感到良心不安，內心過意不去」的意思。讀者們，你有否曾因媽媽叨唸你兩句就心情不好而對媽媽吼叫過呢？事後是否會感到良心不安而覺得對不起媽媽呢？用下句話對媽媽說吧：I feel guilty because I yelled at you. Please forgive me.

不用擔心媽媽聽不懂，她看著你的表情就懂啦。Your guilty look says it all.

小試身手

38. 他被法官判決毀損公物罪。

_____

(39) break the silence（46段）

A few minutes later, it was John once again who broke the silence...

幾分鐘以後，還是約翰打破了沉默……

解析

把「靜默；沉寂」（the silence）看作一堵牆，產生阻絕，造成閉塞，無法溝通。怎麼辦？當然要有人主動挺身而出，打破（break）這堵沉默之牆。除了破牆，還有「破冰」。有些場面局勢，常常因彼此不夠了解或者各持己見而僵在那裡，就像堅硬凍結的「冰（ice）」。如果不想長此僵下去，也需要有人能率先破冰（break the ice），也就是想辦法「打破僵局」。

小試身手

39. 他打破緘默，提出一個替代方案。

_____

---

(40) with tremendous remorse 非常之痛悔自責（47段）

He thanked me, but said to me with tremendous remorse...

他謝謝我，但感慨萬千地向我說……

解析

remorse 為「痛悔；自責」之意，是所謂的抽象名詞。英文有個通則，即抽象名詞置於介詞 with 之後，具副詞的作用（with ＋抽象名詞 ＝ 副詞）。因此，with remorse 即相當於 remorsefully 這個副詞，而 with tremendous remorse 也就和 very remorsefully 相近。

小試身手

40. 他面無愧色地說（臉不紅氣不喘地說）犧牲有時是成功不可或缺的
一部份。

_____

(41) feel chilled to the bone（48段）

When I got home that day, I felt chilled to the bone.
當天，當我回家的時候，我感到好冷。

解析

chilled to the bone「冷到骨子裡了」，還能不冷嗎？不過讀者也應能體會，
這裡不見得是指外在天氣的寒冷，而是心裡那種「淒冷」、「頹喪」的感覺。

小試身手

41. 因為衣著單薄，我一進到開著冷氣的辦公室感到寒冷透骨。

_____

小試身手解答

1. He's such a busybody. He is always poking his nose into things he is not supposed to know.

2. I found it hard to forget about her.

3. The building is in its final stage of construction.

4. The country's already bad economic situation took a turn for the worse because of the war.

5. If it were not for the decreasing number of giant pandas, we would not know how serious a threat human civilization poses to their survival.

6. It wasn't long before he stood up again and made the announcement.

7-1. He was quite displeased when I raised the subject with him.

7-2. I just didn't have the heart to tell her how bad her condition was.

8. Tips from a reliable source helped the police track down the suspect quickly.

9. Taipei is making arrangements for the international conference to be held here in October of this year.

10. A: Can I pick the apples which grow over the fence and into my yard?

    B: I suppose you can justifiably do so.

11. He was obviously taken aback when I exposed his scheme.

12. I was thrown into a paralyzing panic.

13. The detective's investigation shed more light on the case.

14. He successfully acted the part of a relief pitcher and helped his team win its first game.

15. The anti-war campaign was in full swing during the sixties.

16. It suddenly occurred to me that I had a friend from college who lived in this town.

17. By some strange twist of fate, I was assigned a seat next to Harry Potter.

18-1. The pile of books on the desk gave me a headache.

18-2. The sight of the broken windows almost gave me heart attack.

19-1. This book is twice as thick as the one in your hand.

19-2. This piece of metal weighs five times as much as that one.

20-1. These things cost me a fortune.

20-2. Before it dropped, my stock had been going way up for days.

21. She became famous for blowing the whistle on her company's illegal marketing practices.

22. The vivid description of how the vampire took care of his victim made my hair stand on end.

23. He's a man of integrity. You can't possibly buy him off.

24. This necklace was a gift from her. I wouldn't part with it for any price.

25. Whatever wrong you do in this life will come back to haunt you in the afterlife.

26. He believes in high tech. You can always hear him singing the praises of it.

27. I'm so sorry. I don't know how I can make amends for the damage I've done to your reputation.

28. While most young men of his age were working hard to achieve success in their careers, he fooled around with fairweather friends.

29. He promised to accept whatever idea I came up with.

30. Though a little exposure to sunlight can be healthy, too much of it causes skin cancer.

31. Please forgive me—I'm not the man I was.

32. He admitted to having used the drug two or three times and expressed deep regret for it.

33-1. The insect was eaten alive by the lizard.

33-2. Hundreds of wounded captives were buried alive.

33-3. It is required that the fugitives be captured alive.

34. No matter how hard I work on math, I always get a failing grade.

35-1. I accidentally got chewing gum stuck in my hair.

35-2. Tape is sticky to the touch.

36. I clung to the tree trunk and drifted with the currents till I was saved.

37. I consider myself unworthy to continue in that capacity.

38. He was found guilty of vandalism by the court judge.

39. He was the first to break the silence by venturing an alternative plan.

40. He said, without a sign of remorse on his face, that sacrifice is sometimes an indispensable part of success.

41. Being thinly clad, I felt chilled to the bone on entering the air-conditioned office.

A Proper Grasp of Numbers
對數字正確的認識

1-5　　老王去世了，我是看報才知道的，他和我當年是大學商學系的同班同學，畢業以後，兩個人都成了億萬富翁。我們常常見面，有的時候也免不了會互相吹捧一番，畢竟有億萬家產的人也不多。

　　老王說我和他有一個共同的特徵，那就是我們對數字非常敏感，因此我們會感覺到美國利率可能漲，澳洲幣值可能跌，我們更會知道我們設廠的時候該投多少資金下去，該向銀行貨多少錢。說實話，這些事情，多少要靠一些天分，我常看到一些人雇用了一批所謂的財務專家使用了大批電腦程式，我和老王就憑著我們的經驗和直覺，輕而易舉地打敗了這些號稱專家所用的電腦。

　　老王最近很少和我們見面，聽說他已失去賺錢興趣了。我仍在忙自己的事業，沒有時間去問他怎麼一回事。

　　老王的追悼會由他兒子辦的，我和太太坐定以後，發現禮堂的第一排留給家人坐，後面的兩排卻寫了「恩人席」，我左想右想，想不

CD2-2

◇ billionaire (n.) 億萬富翁 (註：此字由 billion 而來，而一個 billion 為「十億」。)
◇ pat (v.) 拍打
◇ observe (v.) 說道
◇ sensitive (adj.) 敏感的；靈敏的
◇ interest rate (s) 利率
◇ invest (v.) 投資
◇ intuition (n.) 直覺
◇ gift (n.) 天資；天賦
◇ financial expert (n.) 理財專家

1-5
CD2-1

Old Wang is dead—I saw the news in the paper. He and I went
to business school together, and both of us became billionaires after
graduating. We used to meet together all the time, and we couldn't
help patting each other on the back every now and then—after all,
there aren't many billionaires in the world.

Old Wang once observed that he and I shared a common
characteristic: we were both very sensitive to numbers. Hence, we
could feel when American interest rates were likely to rise, or when
the Australian dollar might fall. When we built factories, we knew
exactly how much money we should invest ourselves and how much
we should borrow from the bank. To be honest, this sort of intuition
is more of a gift than a learnable skill. I've often seen people hire
teams of so-called financial experts to design lots of fancy computer
models, but they were never a match for me and Old Wang—by
simply relying on our instincts and experience, we never had any
trouble besting them.

Old Wang didn't meet with us much during the time before he died.
I heard he'd lost his interest in making money. But I was still too
busy with my career to ask him to explain why.

The memorial service for Old Wang was arranged by his son. After
my wife and I had sat down, we noticed that behind the first row of
the hall, which had been reserved for family members, there were

◇ computer model 電腦模式
◇ match(n.)對手;敵手
◇ best(v.)勝過;贏過;強過
◇ career(n.)事業;(人生的)志業
◇ memorial service 追思儀式;告別式
◇ reserve(v.)保留;預留

通老王有什麼恩人，像他這種賺大錢的人，該有個「仇人席」還差不多。

典禮開始以前，一輛校車開到了，幾位老師帶了一些學生下車，老王的兒子趕緊去招待，令大家不解的是：這些老師和學生大剌剌地坐進了恩人席。

6-10　　謎底終於解開了，追悼會中最有趣的一段，是老王生前的錄音，他在病榻之上，將他晚年的故事錄了下來，我現在就我的記憶所及，將老王的敘述記錄如下：

「一年以前，我有一天在台北街道等路燈變綠，忽然發現一個小孩子糊裡糊塗地穿越紅燈，一時交通大亂，一連串汽車緊急煞車的聲音，將那個小孩子嚇壞了，可是他好像仍要往前走，我只好衝上去將他一把拉了回來。

「孩子緊緊地拉著我的手不放，我問他名字，他說了，可是問不出來他家在哪裡，我和司機商量的結果，決定帶他到附近的派出所去。

◇ mark（v.）標示；做記號
◇ benefactor（n.）恩人
◇ sedan（n.）私家轎車
◇ rush（v.）衝；快步向前
◇ mystery（n.）玄妙難解的事情；奧秘；謎
◇ solve（v.）破解
◇ narrative（n.）敘述；述說
◇ blunder（v.）誤闖

two rows marked off with signs reading "Benefactors' Seats". No matter how I racked my brain, I couldn't figure out who Old Wang's benefactors could possibly be—a man as rich as he'd been might just as well have reserved "Enemies' Seats" instead.

Before the ceremony began, a sedan pulled up, and a few teachers led several students out of it. Old Wang's son rushed to greet them, and to the amazement of all, the teachers and students sat down smack dab in the middle of the benefactors' seats.

The mystery was eventually solved in the most interesting part of the memorial service, a recording Old Wang had made while he was still alive. As he lay on his sickbed, he recorded the story of the last year of his life. What follows is what I remember of Old Wang's narrative:

6-10

"A year ago, I was waiting at a stoplight on a Taipei street corner one day when suddenly I saw a little boy blunder out into the road, oblivious to the red light. Pandemonium broke out. The squeal of a string of cars slamming on their brakes terrified the boy, but it looked like he intended to keep moving forward. I had no choice but to rush out and pull him back.

"The boy held my hand tightly and wouldn't let go. I asked him his name, and he told me, but I couldn't get him to say where he lived.

◇ oblivious（adj.）渾然不覺的（常接介詞 to 以表示「對……渾然不覺」）
◇ squeal（n.）（尖銳刺耳的）吱吱聲（如輪胎磨擦地面所發出的聲音）

◇ intend（v.）打算；意圖
◇ slam（v.）（尤指用力、重重地）踩；打；撞；甩；摔

「派出所的警員告訴我,有一所智障中心曾打電話來,說他們有一個智障的孩子走失了,他們有他的名字,比對之下,果真是他,我打了電話去,告訴負責人孩子找到了。那裡的人高興極了。

「孩子仍拉著我的手不放,我反正沒有事做,決定送他去。

11-15　　「我從此變成了這所智障中心的座上客,我常去智障中心,也是出於自私心理,我們這種有錢人,一輩子都對別人疑神疑鬼,有人對我好,我就會懷疑他是衝著我有錢來的,唯獨在這所智障中心,孩子們絕對不知道我是何許人也。最令我感到安慰的是,中心的老師也把我當成普通人看,去中心做義工的人不少,很多人顯然認出了我,可是誰也不大驚小怪。

「我發現這所智障中心雖然有政府的補助,可是開銷極大,因為要

◇ consult(v.)商量;商議(註:此字後面常接介詞 with)
◇ mentally handicapped 智障的
◇ retarded(adj.)發展遲緩的
◇ overjoyed(adj.)大喜的;歡欣的
◇ escort(v.)護送

◇ guest of honor 貴賓
◇ terribly(adv.)非常之……;極為……(註:本字在此處表「程度」,相當於中文「非常之……」或「極為……」,一般用以指負面的情況。)
◇ distrustful(adj.)不信任的

After consulting with my driver, I decided to take him to the local police station.

"The officer there told me a center for the mentally handicapped had called to say they'd had a retarded boy wander off. He'd written down the boy's name, and it proved to be the same as what the boy I found had told me. I called the children's center to tell them we'd found their boy. They were overjoyed at the news.

"The boy was still holding onto my hand. I decided to escort him back myself, since in any case I didn't have anything else to do.

"After that, I became the guest of honor at the center. Part of the reason I went there was selfish—you see, we wealthy people are always terribly distrustful of others: when people are kind to us, we suspect they're only doing it for our money. But at this center for the mentally handicapped, the kids literally had no idea who I was. And the most comforting thing was that the teachers there also saw me as an ordinary man. There were many volunteers at the center, and it was obvious that a lot of them recognized me, but no one made a big deal about it.

"I soon learned that although the center was subsidized by the government, their costs were quite high because of the large number of teachers they had to hire. So I decided to donate some money

11-15

◇ suspect (v.) 懷疑
◇ literally (adv.) 幾乎；簡直；實際上
◇ comforting (adj.) 令人安慰的
◇ ordinary (adj.) 平凡的；一般的
◇ recognize (v.) 認得
◇ subsidize (v.) 補助；補貼
◇ government (n.) 政府
◇ donate (v.) 捐款

請很多老師的緣故，我決定送一筆錢給他們。沒想到那位負責人不肯拿這麼多錢，他說需要錢的公益團體非常多，他的原則是不要有太多的錢，因此他只肯收一半，他勸我將另一半捐給別的團體去。

「對我來講，這是第一次知道有人會感到錢太多，我過去從來沒有這種想法。

「有一天，有一個小孩快樂地告訴我，他們種的盆栽都賣掉了，每盆多少錢？這個小子居然說『一塊錢』，旁邊的一個老師很難為情，他告訴我，這些孩子的智商都在四十左右，大概是幼稚園程度，他說很多智障的孩子一臉聰明像，有時看不出有任何問題，最好測試的方法就是問他有關數字的問題，不相信的話，可以問他年齡，果真這孩子說他現在三歲。

「那位老師又說『王先生，並不是每個人都像你這樣對數字有觀念，這個孩子固然對數字一竅不通，就以我們這些人，其實也都不知道怎樣賺錢。人家捐來的錢，我們只會放在銀行裡。』」

◇ charity (n.) 慈善機構
◇ principle (n.) 原則
◇ occur (v.) 使(某人)想起(與 to 連用)
◇ announce (v.) 宣佈

to them. To my amazement, the center director refused to accept such a large sum. There were a lot of charities that needed money, he said, so he avoided having too much of it on principle. Thus, he only accepted half of the money, urging me to donate the rest to other charities.

"That was the first time I'd ever met anyone who thought there was such a thing as having too much money. It was an idea that had never occurred to me before.

"One day, one of the children happily announced that all the potted plants he and his classmates had planted had been sold. "How much a pot?" I asked. The little fellow replied, "One kuai.(buck)" A teacher standing by told me with some embarrassment that these kids had IQs in the neighborhood of forty, about a kindergarten level. A lot of mentally handicapped children looked perfectly intelligent— sometimes you couldn't tell they had a problem just by looking at them. The best way to test their intelligence was to ask them a question about numbers. If I didn't believe him, he said, I could ask the boy how old he was. Sure enough, he said he was three years old.

"The teacher went on to say, 'Mr. Wang, not everybody understands numbers the way you do. Of course these kids don't know a thing about numbers, but it isn't just them—none of us teachers knows how to make money either. We just take what people donate and put it in the bank.'

◇ potted plant(s)盆景；盆栽植物
◇ embarrassment(n.)難為情；不好意思

◇ intelligent(adj.)聰明的；有智慧的；智商高的

16-20　「當天晚上，我的總經理給我看我們最近的業績，我在一個月之內，又賺了幾百萬台幣，我賺了這些錢有何意義？我開始懷疑起來。

　　「對一個沒有什麼錢的人來講，賺錢可以增加安全感，對我而言，可說是毫無意義。像我這種年紀的人，還要不斷地再賺幾百萬，居然有人說我對數字有概念，我覺得我對數字才真是毫無正確的認識，賺了這麼多錢，還要拚老命賺錢，我覺得我和那些智障兒，其實沒有什麼不同。

　　「我唯一的兒子很有出息，不需要我的財產，我留了一個零頭給他，其餘的錢，我成立了一個基金會，所有的財產都進入了這個基金會，專門做慈善工作。當年我從社會上賺的錢，又回到了社會。

　　「我自認我現在對數字有正確的看法。」

　　追悼會完了以後，我和我太太走回汽車，車上的大哥大響了，我

◇ general manager 總經理
◇ performance (n.) 表現（此處可以引申為「營運」、「營收」）
◇ significance (n.) 重大的意義；重要性
◇ sense of security 安全感
◇ prime (n.)（指人生）盛年時期
◇ numerically (adv.) 數字（方面）地
◇ challenged (adj.) 殘障的（婉語）

"That night, my general manager showed me a report on our recent company performance: I'd made another several million this past month. But what was the significance of all this money I was making? I began to doubt whether there was any at all.

"If a man has very little, making money can give him a greater sense of security, but I think it's fair to say that it's meaningless for someone like me. I was well past my prime, yet I never stopped working for those few extra millions... and people said I understood numbers? I felt like I was the numerically challenged one. I'd made all that money, yet I was still working my tail off to make more. I felt like I was really no different from those retarded children.

"My only son was perfectly capable of making his own way in the world—he didn't need my fortune. I left a small portion of it to him and used the rest to establish a foundation devoted to charitable work. The money I made from society is now back where it belongs—in society.

"I believe I now have a proper grasp of numbers."

After the memorial, my wife and I walked back to our car. The car

---

◇ perfectly (adv.) 非常之……；十分地（此字的本義為「完美地」，此處為引申用法）
◇ portion (n.) 部份
◇ establish (v.) 成立；創設
◇ foundation (n.) 基金會
◇ charitable work 慈善工作
◇ grasp (n.) 了解；理解
◇ memorial (n.) 追思會；追悼會

的總經理很高興地告訴我，香港的一筆生意成交了，我又賺進了一千萬。

21-25　車外是個萬里無雲的大好天，氣溫一定在攝氏三十四度左右，我的司機小李是墾丁那一帶的年輕人。我突發奇想，問他，「小李，你想不想去海水浴場游泳？」小李嚇了一跳，不知如何回答才好，我索性告訴他，我今天不上班了。他可以痛痛快快地游泳，小李左謝右謝，他說他將我們送回家以後，就騎機車去淡水，我可以想像得到這個小子穿著汗衫短褲騎機車的神氣樣子。

　　我請小李停車，太太被我拉下了車，我要和她輕鬆地找一家飯館吃午飯，小李受寵若驚地要離開以前，我敲敲前面的車窗，提醒他的游泳褲就放在車子前面的小櫃子裡，我早就發現這件事，所以我才知道小李是個游泳迷，隨時隨地想找個機會去游泳。小李被我發現他的秘密，非常不好意思。

◇ close（v.）完成；了結
◇ degree（n.）度（註：幾何學裡的角度，科學裡的溫度，甚至一般場合的程度，都可使用本字。）
◇ Celsius ['sɛlsɪəs]（n.）攝氏溫度制（原本為發明此數值制度以測量溫度的瑞典天文學家名字，現用以指這個制度。）
◇ guard（n.）留神；戒備
◇ content（n.）滿足
◇ profusely（adv.）大量地；豐盛地
◇ dashing（adj.）瀟灑的；帥氣的（a dashing figure 相當於中文的「英姿煥發的模樣」）
◇ tank top（n.）背心

phone rang; it was my general manager. He happily told me we'd just closed a deal in Hong Kong that would make me another ten million.

Outside the car, it was a beautiful day, without a cloud in the sky— **21-25** it must have been about 34 degrees Celsius. My driver, little Li, was a young man from the Kenting area. Suddenly I had a great idea: I asked him, "Little Li, how would you like to go for a swim at the beach?" Caught off guard, Little Li wasn't quite sure how to answer. I told him I wasn't going to work today, so he could swim to his heart's content. He thanked me profusely and said that after he dropped me off at my house, he'd ride his scooter up to Danshui. I could imagine what a dashing figure he'd cut riding his scooter in his tank top and shorts.

I had Little Li park the car, then led my wife out; I wanted to stroll around looking for a restaurant where we could eat together. As Little Li, overwhelmed by his good fortune, was about to leave, I knocked on the front car window and reminded him that his swim trunks were in the glove compartment. I'd discovered their hiding place long ago, which was how I knew Little Li loved to go swimming wherever and whenever he could. Little Li was mortified that I'd discovered his secret.

◇ stroll(v.)漫步；閒逛
◇ overwhelmed(adj.)(指情緒)到不可遏止之地步的(如「哀慟逾恆」就可寫為(be)overwhelmed with grief)
◇ swim trunks(男士的)泳褲(用複數型)

◇ glove compartment(n.)汽車前座的櫃子
◇ mortified(adj.)羞愧的；不好意思的

　　我和太太找了一家吃牛肉麵的地方，老闆問我們吃大碗、中碗或小碗，我們都點了小碗，再加了一盤小菜。

　　我太太說：「老頭子，麵只能吃小碗了，錢卻要拚命地賺，我問你，我們賺這麼多錢有什麼用？連吃都吃不下了。」

　　我不理她，她知道我要怎樣處理我的財產，我和老王一樣，對數字都有正確的認識，我會正確地處理我賺來的錢，錢從哪裡來，就應回到哪裡去，我總不能被人笑成了智障兒。

◇ place (n.) 店 (此字常用以指提供吃喝的場所，「披薩店」即可用 a pizza place 表示之)

◇ medium (adj.) 中型的
◇ side dish 小菜
◇ ignore (v.) 不理；忽視

My wife and I went into a little beef noodles place. The host asked us if we wanted small, medium or large bowls. We both ordered smalls, along with a little side dish.

My wife said, "Old man, why do you work so hard to make money when all you can eat is a small bowl of noodles? What good does it do you to make so much money when we can't even finish our food?"

I ignored her—she knew how I was going to dispose of my money. Just like Old Wang, I now had a proper grasp of numbers. I would do the right thing with the money I'd made: money should go back where it came from. Besides, I'd be a laughingstock if I was no wiser than a retarded child.

◇ dispose（v.）去除掉；處理；解決（本字的後面常接 of 這個介詞）
◇ laughingstock（n.）笑柄；笑譚

（1）pat each other on the back 稱兄道弟；熱絡套交情（1段）

We used to meet together all the time, and we couldn't help patting each other on the back every now and then—after all, there aren't many billionaires in the world.

我們常常見面，有的時候也免不了會互相吹捧一番，畢竟有億萬家產的人也不多。

解析

動詞 pat 的意思為用手「拍打」，所以 pat each other 是「我拍打你，你拍打我」，問題是拍身體的那個部位呢？熟朋友間見了面，熱絡套套交情，彼此相互拍拍背部（on the back），稱兄道弟一番。綜合起來，pat each other on the back 指的就是「稱兄道弟」或「熱絡套交情」。而 a pat on the back 則表示稱讚嘉許之意。

此外還有三個讀者需要知道的東西，一個是 couldn't help，是「禁不住」，另一個是 every now and then，指「偶而」、「有時」，最後一個是 after all，相當於中文「畢竟」、「到底」。

小試身手

1. 工作做得很好。你值得鼓勵一下。

＿＿＿＿＿＿＿＿＿＿＿＿＿＿＿＿＿＿＿＿＿＿＿＿＿

（2）to be honest 說實話；說真的；坦白講（2段）

To be honest, this sort of intuition is more of a gift than a learnable skill.

說實話，這些事情，多少要靠一些天分。

解析

to be honest 是慣用語，常放在句子開頭，來向聽者表明，接下所說的是發

自內心，符合事實的真心話。比如「說實在的，技能比學歷來得重要。」

本重點另外一個學習焦點為 more of a gift than a learnable skill，請注意這是一種比較的結構，就字面而言是「更屬天份」(more of a gift)，「而非可以學得來的技巧」(than a learnable skill)，演變到最後就成了「是……而非……」。

小試身手

2. 今天長城有的是觀光價值而非軍事用途。

_____

（3）never a match for... 絕對不是……的對手（2段）

I've often seen people hire teams of so-called financial experts to design lots of fancy computer models, but they were never a match for me and Old Wang...

我常看到一些人雇用了一批所謂的財務專家使用了大批電腦程式，我和老王……，輕而易舉地打敗了這些專家……

解析

(a) match 為名詞，為「實力相當，可以相匹敵的人或物」，後面常接介詞 for。因此 a match for... 即是「……的敵手、對手」而 never a match for... 則表示「絕非……的對手」，用它來表達「輕而易舉地打敗」，譯法很巧妙。

小試身手

3. 贗品無論在外觀和真品多接近，在品質上絕非真品的對手（絕無法與之相比）。

_____

（4） mark（ed）off （4段）

... there were two rows marked off with signs reading "Benefactors' Seats".

後面的兩排卻寫了「恩人席」。

解析

marker 這個英文單字，就是我們拿來劃線、寫字、作記號的「麥克筆」。所以片語 mark off 就是以劃記劃線的方式「標示出來」、「區隔出來」。

譯文裡一口氣出現兩個分詞片語：marked off with signs 和 reading "Benefactors' Seats"。它們分別是以下兩個子句精簡過來的，讀者可以花些時間用心思考：

which were marked off with signs → marked off with signs

which read "Benefactors' Seats" → reading "Benefactors' Seats"

> **小試身手**
>
> 4. 公園的這一區被標示出來，供人們讓狗在此活動。
>
> _____

（5） rack one's brain 苦思；絞盡腦汁（4段）

No matter how I racked my brain, I couldn't figure out who Old Wang's benefactors could possibly be.

我左想右想，想不通老王有什麼恩人。

解析

從人體解剖的角度看，brain 指的是「腦部」，為單數名詞。rack 本來是一種用來把人拉到骨頭斷掉的酷刑刑具，所以，當成動詞使用時，表示用力使

用或折磨的意思。例如 rack my brain（絞盡腦汁）和 nerve-racking（神經折磨）都是 rack 常見用例。

小試身手

5. 考那個試是我生平最緊張的事。

_____

---

(6) sit down smack dab in the middle（of）坐到……正中央來（5段）

... and to the amazement of all, the teachers and students sat down smack dab in the middle of the benefactors' seats.

令大家不解的是：這些老師和學生大剌剌地坐進了恩人席。

解析

原本的片語為 sit（down）in the middle（of）... ，意義為「坐在……中間」，在 in the middle（of）... 之前加個 right 成為 sit（down）right in the middle（of）... ，以強調「就坐在……正中間」、「剛好就坐在……中央」。譯文更加通俗化，口語化，用 smack dab 取代 right，讓片語成為 sit down smack dab in the middle（of）...（大剌剌的坐在正中間）。口語英文有趣，但並不好學。原因無他，口語英文使用在實際語言情境中，非母語環境裡很難學得自然。

小試身手

6. 看，那可憐的傢伙額頭的正中間長了好大一個青春痘！

_____

（7）**wait at a stoplight** 等紅燈（7段）

　　　（be）**oblivious to...** 沒注意……；無視……

A year ago, I was waiting at a stoplight on a Taipei street corner one day when suddenly I saw a little boy blunder out into the road, oblivious to the red light.

一年以前，我有一天在台北街道等路燈變綠，忽然發現一個小孩子糊裡糊塗地穿越紅燈。

解析

這是一句很好的英譯，讀者不妨集中思考，將以下三者作為學習標的。

第一個是「等路燈變綠」，當然任何人都知道這裡「路燈」其實指的是「交通號誌燈」（stoplight）或（traffic light）。問題是平時掛在嘴邊的「等紅燈」英文怎麼說呢？譯者幫我們解決了這個苦惱，就是 wait at a stoplight 啦。當然，還可用 wait at a red light 或 wait for the light to turn green 來表示，但在一般不用特別強調紅燈綠燈時，用 stoplight 即可。

第二個要學習的是「誤闖馬路」，譯者以 blunder out into the road 來處理，動詞 blunder 指的是「犯錯」，而且是「不明究理地犯錯」。

第三個可學習的東西為 oblivious to...，表示「不注意……」、「無視……」，所以譯文中 oblivious to the red light 即表示「紅燈亮著也視若無睹」、「無視紅燈之存在」。

小試身手

7-1. 我放慢車速，希望在我完全得停住之前變綠燈。

_____

7-2. 他口出穢言，完全無視他就置身公共場所。

_____

（8）**Pandemonium breaks out.**（因情況失控而）天下大亂（7段）

Pandemonium broke out.

一時交通大亂。

解析

pandemonium 指的是妖魔鬼怪群居之處，群魔亂舞之地。如果關不住這些地獄惡客，讓裡頭的魔妖傾巢而出（break out），肆虐作惡，豈不天下大亂，永無寧日？

小試身手

8.　武裝搶匪闖進銀行，隨即天下大亂。

＿＿＿＿＿＿＿＿＿＿＿＿＿＿＿＿＿＿＿＿＿＿＿＿＿＿＿

（9）**slam on the brakes** 猛（急）踩煞車（7段）

The squeal of a string of cars slamming on their brakes terrified the boy, but it looked like he intended to keep moving forward.

一連串汽車緊急煞車的聲音，將那個小孩子嚇壞了，可是他好像仍要往前走。

解析

某人怒氣沖沖，離開房間時順手重重一摔，把房門關起來，這樣子的動作，英文用 slam the door shut 表示。可以想像得到，動詞指的是很用力的「打、拍、擊、甩」。這裡用 slam on the brakes 來表示「猛（急）踩煞車」，真的是生動傳神。

小試身手

9. 計程車司機猛踩煞車時，輪胎發出刺耳尖銳的聲音。

_____

（10）consult with someone 和（某人）商量（8段）

After consulting with my driver, I decided to take him to the local police station.

我和司機商量的結果，決定帶他到附近的派出所去。

解析

既然 talk with 和 speak with 是「和（某人）說話」；converse with 和 chat with 是「和（某人）閒話聊天」；那麼 consult with 自然就是「和（某人）商量」。且把 consult 這個字記住了，意思為「商量」、「商議」。

小試身手

10. 李先生沒有事先和太太商量就做了決定。

_____

（11）wander off 走失（9段）

The officer there told me a center for the mentally handicapped had called to say they'd had a retarded boy wander off.

派出所的警員告訴我，有一所智障中心曾打電話來，說他們有一個智障的孩子走失了。

解析

動詞 wander 作「漫走」、「到處游走」解釋，之後的介副詞有「消失不見」

的意味，所以整個 wander off 作「走失」解。

小試身手

11. 當媽媽在和女店員講價錢時，那個孩子走失了。

_____

（12）be（terribly）distrustful of others 對人（非常）不信任（11段）

Part of the reason I went there was selfish—you see, we wealthy people are always terribly distrustful of others...

我常去智障中心，也是出於自私心理，我們這種有錢人，一輩子都對別人疑神疑鬼。

解析

如果你和英文的接觸史已有點時日，應該知道（-ful）這種型態的形容詞，之前常是（BE）動詞，之後常是（of）這個介詞。例子真的是不勝枚舉，以下就有幾個：be（dis）respectful of..., be mindful of..., be neglectful of..., be scornful of..., be forgetful of...

字典是學英文的利器，你可以到字典裡去查詢以上這些片語的意義和用法，收穫會更多。還有，你有否注意到，這些（-ful）型態的形容詞都是趨向於表示「知性」或「情意」方面的意思。

小試身手

12. 對別人不信任的人對自己也常沒有信心。

_____

---

(13) it is obvious that... 顯然（11段）

There were many volunteers at the center, and it was obvious that a lot of them recognized me, but no one made a big deal about it.

去中心做義工的人不少，很多人顯然認出了我，可是誰也不大驚小怪。

解析

且把 It is obvious that... 當作固定句型來看，當你要表達「（某事）很明顯」時，就把它用出來。比如：「天空烏雲密佈。顯然颱風就快到了。」

讀者在英譯裡還可以學到一句口語 make a big deal about it，譯者用它來傳達「大驚小怪」，非常傳神，因為這個口語的字面含意是「把它（about it）當成（make）一件不得了的大事情（a big deal）」實在有意思吧！對了，介詞除了使用 about，也可改用 out of，效果一樣。在生活中，在影集裡，幾個老外聊天，常冒出一句 Big deal! 讀者不妨猜猜看，大致是什麼意思。

小試身手

13. 天空烏雲密佈。顯然颱風要來了。

_____

(14) on principle 秉持原則；原則上（12段）

There were a lot of charities that needed money, he said, so he avoided having too much of it on principle.

需要錢的公益團體非常多，他的原則是不要有太多的錢。

解析

on principle 在此有「依原則」行事的意味。因此譯文中 he avoided having too much of it on principle 一語即指「依他的行事原則不取過多的錢」。在金錢方面有這種原則而且能堅守的人，當今之世殊少見到吧。

小試身手

14. 她是如此致力於防範全球暖化，所以她原則上拒開休旅車。

_____

(15) in the neighborhood of... 在……左右；在……上下；差不多是……（14段）

A teacher standing by told me with some embarrassment that these kids had IQs in the neighborhood of forty, about a kindergarten level.

旁邊的一個老師很難為情，他告訴我，這些孩子的智商都在四十左右，大概是幼稚園程度。

解析

(the) neighborhood 為「鄰近地帶」、「居家附近地區」。很自然的，片語 in the neighborhood of... 就可引申解釋為「在……左右（上下）」、「差不多是……」。

英文另有 proximity to 和 vicinity of 等詞組也可表示「相近」、「鄰近」的意思。

小試身手

15. 她的年紀嘛，我猜呢，約莫在五十歲上下吧。

_____

(16) the way someone does/did 像某人那樣地……（15段）

Mr. Wang, not everybody understands numbers the way you do.

王先生，並不是每個人都像你這樣對數字有觀念。

解析

這是一種副詞子句，其作用在修飾主要子句的動詞。以英譯句而言，**the way you do** 的修飾對象就是主要子句的動詞 (understands)。其實原句 not everybody understands numbers the way you do 和 not everybody understands numbers as well as you do 兩者相去不遠，但在感覺上 the way you do 更為口語化。

小試身手

16. 如果你喝酒像他這種喝法，你很快就會喝醉。

_____

（17）**don't know a thing about...** 對……一無所知；根本就不懂……（15段）

Of course these kids don't know a thing about numbers, but it isn't just them—none of us teachers knows how to make money either.

這個孩子固然對數字一竅不通，就以我們這些人，其實也都不知道怎樣賺錢。

解析

請把握一個原則，"not... a" 其實就相當於 "no"。所以 don't know a thing about... 和 know nothing about... 一樣，都是「根本不懂……」、「對……一無所知」的意思。由此推想，中文的「略知一二」該怎麼說呢？

小試身手

17. 我對草藥略知一二。

_____

（18） what is the significance of... （某事）意義何在？（16段）

But what was the significance of all this money I was making? I began to doubt whether there was any at all.

我賺了這些錢有何意義？我開始懷疑起來。

解析

significance 是「意義」或「重要性」的意思，和它相近的有 purpose 或其他名詞。原著中文為「我賺了這些錢有何意義？」如果你想把重點放在「賺」，也可以把句子寫為 But what was the purpose of my making all this money?

小試身手

18. 投資那麼多錢在一個污染環境的工業有何好處？

_____

（19） be well past one's prime 已過盛年（17段）

I was well past my prime, yet I never stopped working for those few extra millions... and people said I understood numbers?

像我這種年紀的人，還要不斷地再賺幾百萬，居然有人說我對數字有概念。

解析

名詞 prime 指人或事的發展達到巔峰、臻於全盛。

譯者以 I was well past my prime 來詮釋「像我這種年紀的人」，表示當事人青春已逝，年華不再，已經早過了人生的黃金歲月。這裡的 well 是加強 past 的語氣，平常也可不用，例如：He used to be a great pitcher, but now he's past his prime.（他曾經是個很棒的捕手，但現在已經過了他的黃金時期了。）

小試身手

19. 他在發現盛年已過時隨即退休。

_____

(20) work one's tail off 辛苦勞累地工作（17段）

I'd made all that money, yet I was still working my tail off to make more.

賺了這麼多錢，還要拚老命賺錢。

解析

喔，這個片語真好玩。賣力工作，辛苦勞累到尾巴都累斷了，其賣力勞累的程度，可以想見。你覺得不合理嗎？其實大可不必，平常我們不也常說某事的發展或某人的作為讓人「跌破眼鏡」，你真的會以為某人有副眼鏡掉到地上摔破了嗎？英文還有 cry one's eyes out 和 cry one's head off 之類更怪的片語哩。

小試身手

20. 要養活四口之家，我父親得賣力工作。

_____

(21) make one's own way in the world 闖出自己的一片天；事業有成；有出息（18段）

My only son was perfectly capable of making his own way in the world—he didn't need my fortune.

我唯一的兒子很有出息，不需要我的財產。

解析

在 make one's own way in the world 這個片語裡，make one's own way 表示「成功」、「成就」，因此整個片語指的是完全靠自己，不依賴他人扶持而「人生成功」、「事業有成」的意義。

> **小試身手**
>
> 21. 我搞不懂他的資源有限卻能闖出名堂來。
>
> _____

（22）文法：副詞子句（where something belongs）某樣東西原來的歸屬之處（18段）

The money I made from society is now back where it belongs—in society.

當年我從社會上賺的錢，又回到了社會。

解析

從文法的角度看，where something belongs 是一種「地方副詞子句」。就作用上來講，它和讀者們平常看到的如 here, there, upstairs, indoors, in the woods, on the wall, at the station, in the west 之類的「地方副詞」沒有兩樣，都是表達了「地方」、「位置」、「場所」、「方位」的概念，一般作修飾句子的動詞之用。

出國讀書，拿到學位，覺得國外雖好，終究不是生養自己的地方，決定回到自己所從出的地方，貢獻所學，服務人群社會——試試底下題目吧！

> **小試身手**
>
> 22. 我決定回到我原來歸屬之處去貢獻育我的土地。
>
> _____

（23）have a proper grasp of... 對⋯⋯有正確了解（19段）

I believe I now have a proper grasp of numbers.

我自認我現在對數字有正確的看法。

解析

讀者們，如果我把片語裡的 a proper grasp 改成 a good understanding 使之成為 have a good understanding of... ，你是否會覺得頓時豁然開朗呢？說穿了，原片語裡的 grasp 其實就是「領悟」、「了解」的意思，和各位熟悉的 understanding 大致相同。學習英文，要記住一個事實，英文字常是一字多義，grasp 一般作「抓住」解釋雖然沒錯，但是它也可能具備一些其他的意思。其實仔細想想，「了解」這個意思就是從「抓住」延伸過來的。我這樣說，你「抓到」我的意思了嗎？

小試身手

23. 幾乎人人知道金錢的重要性，但是似乎沒有幾個人真正了解錢的價值。

_____

（24）（be）caught off guard 因沒有心理防備而慌了手腳；冷不防（21段）

Caught off guard, Little Li wasn't quite sure how to answer.

小李嚇了一跳，不知如何回答才好。

解析

這是個很漂亮、很值得一學的片語。guard 為「警惕」、「警覺」之類的心理的防禦機制，所以 off guard 的意思就指向撤離了心理的防禦機制，成了「失去警惕」、「沒有警覺」。整個片語 (be)caught off guard 則指的是一種因某事「突如其來而令人難以因應」的狀況。

24. 當被問到那個問題時，他顯然慌了手腳。

_____

(25) to one's heart's content（做某事到）盡興；心滿意足（21段）

I told him I wasn't going to work today, so he could swim to his heart's content.

我索性告訴他，我今天不上班了。他可以痛痛快快地游泳。

解析

做什麼事情（如本文所指的游泳）可以無拘無束，做到讓自己痛快盡興，做到自己覺得心（heart）滿（content）意（heart）足（content）應是人生一大快事。中文的「心滿」和「意足」用字不同，其意義則無異，相對應的英文則以 heart's content 來表現，東西方人種不同，地理相異，在語言思考上卻如此接近，真令人訝異。

25. 既然期末考結束了，我要好好打電動玩具打個夠。

_____

(26) cut a dashing figure（表現出）瀟灑帥氣的模樣（21段）

I could imagine what a dashing figure he'd cut riding his scooter in his tank top and shorts.

我可以想像得到這個小子穿著汗衫短褲騎機車的神氣樣子。

解析

這種英文就真的不好學了，cut a dashing figure 竟會冒出一個「瀟灑帥氣的模樣」的意思來，真是令人一個頭兩個大，就好比一位初學中文的老外，第一次聽到「一個頭兩個大」，也會覺得莫名其妙，不知所云。怎麼辦呢？只好先把它記下，有機會在適當場合利用它，或許可以達到熟能生巧的境界。

小試身手

26. 他穿著西裝，展現出一副很有氣質的模樣。

_____

（27）**What good does it do someone... ?**（某事）對某人何益？（**24**段）

What good does it do you to make so much money when we can't even finish our food?

我們賺這麼多錢有什麼用？連吃都吃不下了。

解析

英文有 do good to someone 和 do someone good 這兩片語，表示「有益某人」、「對某人有好處」。比如：「適量的運動有必要而且對你的健康大有好處。」就可以用這兩個片語表現而寫成：Proper exercise is necessary and will do your health a lot of good.

機靈的讀者也許會想：既然如此，那「對某人有害處」又該如何表現呢？你可以獨立作業或和別人商量，然後到以下小試身手來表現。

小試身手

27. 把你的車子借我一用於你有什麼壞處（於你何損）呢？

_____

（28）no wiser than... 比……聰明不到哪裡去；和……一樣笨（25段）

Besides, I'd be a laughingstock if I was no wiser than a retarded child.
（而且）我總不能被人笑成了智障兒。

解析

讀者要注意這種 no ADJer than... 結構（ADJer 指的是形容詞比較級），以上英譯的 no wiser than... 指的是「沒有比……聰明到哪裡去」，説起來真正的意思是「和……一樣笨」（as stupid as... ）。

請看下例。某甲説：「傑克很懶。」某乙接著説：「他的弟弟傑洛也好不到哪裡。」讀者們應該都知道這裡某乙所言的「……也好不到哪裡。」其實是「……也勤奮不到哪兒去。」

以上兩句以英文表現如下：

A: Jack is lazy.

B: His brother Jarod is no better（than he is）.

小試身手

28. 那個武器和鉛筆一樣小，但威力強大而且能致人於死。

_____

小試身手解答

1. Job well done! You deserve a pat on the back.

2. Today, the Great Wall has more sightseeing value than military usefulness.

3. The fake, however close it is to the original in appearance, is no match for it in quality.

4. This part of the park is marked off for people to let their dogs run around.

5. Taking that test was the most nerve-racking experience of my life.

6. Look, that poor guy has a big zit right smack dab in the middle of his forehead!

7-1. I slowed down, hoping the light would turn green before I had to stop completely.

7-2. He used filthy language, totally oblivious to the fact that he was in a public place.

8. As soon as the armed robbers broke into the bank, pandemonium broke out.

9. The tires squealed as the taxi driver slammed on the brakes.

10. Mr. Li made the decision without consulting with his wife beforehand.

11. The kid wandered off while his mother was bargaining with the saleswoman.

12. Those who are distrustful of others are often unsure of themselves.

13. The sky is full of thick, dark clouds. It is obvious that a typhoon is on its way.

14. She's so dedicated to fighting global warming that she refuses to drive an SUV on principle.

15. I would guess that her age is somewhere in the neighborhood of fifty.

16. You would get drunk very fast if you drank the way he does.

17. I know one or two things about herbal medicine.

18. What's the good of investing so much in an industry that pollutes the environment?

19. He retired soon after he discovered he was past his prime.

20. To support a family of four, my father had to work his tail off.

21. It beats me how he made his own way in the world with such a limited amount of resources.

22. I decided to go back where I belong to serve the land which had nourished me.

23. Almost everybody knows the importance of money, but few seem to have a true grasp of its value.

24. He was obviously caught off guard when the question was put to him.

25. Now that the final exam is over, I can play video games to my heart's content.

26. He really cuts a fine figure in a business suit.

27. What harm would it do you to lend me your car for a while?

28. The weapon is no bigger than a pencil, but it can be powerful and deadly.

My Home
我的家

1-5　　我從師大畢業以後，第一個實習工作是在鄉下做老師，對我這個從小到大在城市長大的人而言，鄉下簡直是天堂，這裡空氣永遠新鮮，天空永遠蔚藍，溪水也永遠乾淨，所以我每天一放學，就到校外去，沿著鄉間的小徑散步。

　　散步的時候，當然會碰到玩耍的小孩子，我發現有幾個小孩子特別地友善，他們不僅和我打招呼，而且也會主動要求我幫他們的忙。

　　有一次，他們的球掉到了一條小溪中間的石頭上，這些小鬼不敢去拿，怕掉到河裡去。我走過，一個小鬼叫我叔叔，然後就請我去撿那個球，我冒著生命的危險去撿了給他們，他們好高興。

　　第二次，問題更嚴重了，他們的球滾到一棵大榕樹下面，那裡躺了一條大黃狗。小鬼們看到了這條大狗，誰也不敢去拿球。我走過，這個撿球的工作又落到我的肩上。我鼓起了勇氣，向大樹走去，同時用友善的眼光看那條大狗，牠不僅沒有對我叫，反而搖起尾巴來了。

CD2-4
◇ rural (adj.) 鄉下的；村野的
◇ heaven (n.) 天堂
◇ azure [ˋæʒɚ] (adj.) 蔚藍的
◇ friendly (adj.) 友好的；和善的

◇ devil (n.) 惡魔 (little devils 就是「小鬼頭；小壞蛋」)
◇ risk (v.) 冒著……危險
◇ banyan tree [ˋbænjən] 榕樹

The first internship I got after graduating from NTNU was as a teacher in a rural town. Before then, I had spent my whole life in the city, so the country felt like heaven to me: the air was always fresh, the sky was always azure, and the stream water was always clean. Each day, as soon as school got out, I'd leave the campus and take a walk along a path through the countryside.

1-5

CD2-3

Naturally, during these walks I'd often run across children at play. I found that a few of them were especially friendly—they'd say hello to me and even come over and ask me for help.

Once, for instance, their ball had fallen onto a rock in the middle of a stream. The little devils were afraid that if they tried to get it themselves, they'd fall into the water. As I walked past, one of them called me Uncle and asked me to pick up the ball. I risked my life to pick it up for them; they were overjoyed.

The problem was more serious the next time. Their ball had rolled under a large banyan tree, where a big yellow dog was lying down. As soon as they saw the dog, none of the little devils would get the ball. Then I walked by, and the burden of retrieving the ball once again fell on my shoulders. I gathered up my courage and walked toward the tree, giving the dog a friendly look. Not only did he not bark at me, he even started wagging his tail.

◇ retrieve (v.) 取回；拿回
◇ shoulder (s) (n.) 肩膀
◇ courage (n.) 勇氣
◇ wag (v.) (指如狗之類的動物) 搖 (尾巴)

當我將球丟給那些頑童的時候，他們給我一個英雄式的歡迎。

我學過一些兒童心理學，當時就感覺這些小孩子一定出自相當幸福的家庭，所以才會對陌生人如此友善，破碎家庭的小孩子多半對人不太信任，絕對不會叫陌生人替他撿球的。

6-10　既然他們對我如此友善，我就一不做，二不休，問他們住在哪裡。孩子們異口同聲地請我同他們一起回家。我一路跟著他們，這才發現我倒楣了，因為其中最小的一個還要我揹。

出乎意料的是，這些孩子住在一家孤兒院裡，現在當然不流行叫孤兒院，而叫兒童中心，進入了院門，孩子們溜得無影無蹤，和別的孩子們瘋去了。

一位修女和我打招呼，也謝謝我陪孩子們玩。不一會兒，那個最小的小孩出現了，他拉了我的手，帶我去看他的臥室，因為他仍是幼稚園學生，所以似乎床單等等都有動物或卡通人物的圖樣，他也有一個

◇ a hero's welcome 英雄式的歡迎　　◇ a piggyback ride 讓人背者走
◇ child psychology 兒童心理學　　　◇ totally(adv.) 完全地；整個地
◇ ordinarily(adv.) 一般地；平常地　◇ orphanage(n.) 孤兒院
◇ broken(adj.) 破碎的　　　　　　　◇ fashionable(adj.) 時尚的；流行的

When I returned the ball to the kids, they gave me a hero's welcome.

I've studied some child psychology in the past, and at the time I thought that these children must have come from very happy families—otherwise they wouldn't have been so friendly to a stranger. Ordinarily, children from broken families didn't trust strangers much, and they wouldn't even think of asking a stranger to get a ball for them.

Since they were so friendly to me, I figured there was no harm in asking them where they lived. With one voice they invited me home with them. I followed them there, discovering too late that it wasn't my lucky day—the littlest child wanted a piggyback ride.

6-10

I was totally surprised to find that the children lived in an orphanage. Of course, nowadays it isn't fashionable to call them orphanages—they're called children's centers. As soon as we set foot inside the gate, the kids scattered without a trace, off to play with the other kids.

A nun greeted me and thanked me for playing with the children. Not long afterward, the littlest child appeared; he tugged at my hand and led me to his room. Because he was still in kindergarten, his sheets and other possessions all seemed to have animals or cartoon characters on them. He had a little closet, too, where he stored his

◇ scatter (v.) 散開
◇ trace (n.) 痕跡
◇ tug (v.) 拉；扯
◇ kindergarten (n.) 幼稚園
◇ cartoon character (n.) 卡通人物
◇ closet (n.) 衣櫃

小櫃子，裡面藏著他的一些寶貝。

就這麼短短的接觸，我發現我的褲子口袋裡多了兩顆玻璃彈珠，四顆小石子和一條蚯蚓。

我終於了解為什麼孩子們生活在一所兒童中心裡，仍然會如此快樂，而且對陌生人如此友善，原因很簡單，他們所接觸的人都是好人，他們知道，如果他們有什麼問題，我們這些人總會幫他們的忙。我們雖然不是他們的親人，他們卻總把我們視為親人。孩子病了，我被捉去開車送他們去看醫生，孩子功課不好，我又被抓去做家教。不僅如此，他們也都非常尊重我們，我們這些叔叔伯伯阿姨們，隨時要抱這些孩子們，可是也都隨時可以管他們，至於修女們，更有權威了。他們什麼事都去找修女，也心甘情願地接受修女們的管教。

11-15　實習完了以後，我回到台北市，在一所國中教書，學生全都來自中產階級的家庭，大多數都很正常，但有一個例外，這個孩子老是有點心不在焉，功課也不太好。

有一天，我發現他沒有來上課，打電話去他家，他媽媽說他已經離

◇ treasure(s)(n.)寶貝；珍愛的東西
◇ contact(n.)聯絡；接觸
◇ tutor(v.)個別教授
◇ hug(v.)擁抱
◇ reprimand(v.)訓誡；斥責

◇ authority(n.)權威
◇ submit(v.)(後面接介詞 to 以表示)接受
◇ discipline(n.)管教
◇ internship(n.)實習
◇ vast(adj.)浩大的；眾多的

treasures.

After our short encounter, I discovered that the contents of my pockets had increased by two marbles, four pebbles and a worm.

I finally understood why these kids were so happy and so friendly to strangers despite their living in a children's center. The reason was simple: all the people they came in contact with were good people. They knew that we would always help them whenever they had problems. Although we weren't family, they saw us as family. If children got sick, I'd be asked to take them to see the doctor; if a child did poorly in school, I'd be asked to tutor him. Moreover, they all had great respect for us—at any given moment, we uncles and aunts could hug them, but we could also reprimand them. As for the nuns, they had even more authority. The kids would go to the nuns for everything, and they willingly submitted to their discipline.

After I finished the internship, I went back to Taipei, where I taught at a junior high. The students all came from middle-class homes, and the vast majority of them were perfectly normal, but there was one exception. This boy's mind always seemed to be elsewhere, and his schoolwork left something to be desired.

One day, I noticed that he hadn't shown up for class. I called his house, and his mom said he'd run away from home. He'd disappeared

11-15

◇ majority (n.) 多數
◇ normal (adj.) 正常的
◇ schoolwork (n.) 課業；學業
◇ desire (v.) 渴求；想望 (left something to be desired 相當於中文的「很有待加強」)
◇ disappear (v.) 失蹤；不見

開家了,又說他曾經失蹤一次,事後又回來了。聽她的口氣,她好像不太擔心。

第二天,我接到派出所的電話,他們在火車站裡看到我的學生在裡面睡覺,帶他去派出所,他堅決不肯告訴警察他住的地方,也不肯告訴他們他的父母是誰。可是從他的制服上,可以知道他就讀的學校。因為制服上繡了他的名字,他們很快就查出我是他的級任導師。警察叫我立刻去派出所。

警察告訴我,這個在火車站過夜的孩子絕不是窮人的孩子,因為他的身上有進入公寓的電腦卡片,也有幾千塊錢,他們完全不懂,既然他住在要刷卡才能進入的大廈裡,為什麼晚上會跑到火車站去過夜?現在既然導師來了,警察就將孩子交給了我,當然他們強調我一定要將孩子送回家。

我帶他去吃燒餅油條,雖然他不肯告訴警察他住哪裡,可是我知道,因為學校裡的學生資料上有他的住址。儘管他老大不願意,在我一再勸說以後,他答應由我陪他回家,可是他希望我們下午才去。

◇ sound(v.)(某人)口氣(聽起來)……
◇ stitch(v.)縫
◇ uniform(n.)制服
◇ perplexed(adj.)困惑的;糊塗不清的
◇ swipe(v.)刷(卡)
◇ student mentor 學生導師
◇ emphasize(v.)強調
◇ include(v.)包括

like this once before, she said, but then he came back again. She didn't sound overly worried.

The next day, I got a call from the police station. They had seen my student sleeping in the train station and taken him back to the station with them, but he refused to tell them where he lived, and he wouldn't tell them who his parents were either. But they could tell from his uniform what school he went to, and because his name was stitched on the uniform, they quickly found out that I was the student mentor for his grade. They asked me to come to the station immediately.

At the station, the officers told me that this boy who had spent the night in the train station was obviously not from a poor family, judging by the electronic apartment access card and several thousand yuan in cash that he was carrying. They were perplexed as to why he would go spend the night in a train station when he lived in a building you had to swipe a card to get into. Now that I, his student mentor, had arrived, the police turned the boy over to me, emphasizing, of course, that I had to take him home.

I took him out for sesame seed cakes and fried breadsticks. Even though he wouldn't tell the police where he lived, I knew perfectly well—his address was included in the student information kept by the school. Notwithstanding his great reluctance, after a great deal of effort, I finally persuaded him to let me take him home. But he wanted to wait until afternoon to go.

◇ reluctance (n.) 勉強不願　　　　◇ persuade (v.) 說服
◇ effort (n.) 努力

16-20　　果真他住在一座非常講究的大廈，進大門要刷卡，連乘電梯都要刷卡，他的家也很舒服，他有一輛新的腳踏車、昂貴的音響和電腦設備，表示他是那種什麼都有的孩子，我們去的時候，他媽媽不在家，我事先曾打電話告訴她，孩子已經找到了。

　　孩子告訴我，他爸媽離婚，他和媽媽住，從家裡照片上來看，他的媽媽很漂亮。我問他媽媽有沒有工作，他說有的，我又問他媽媽在哪裡工作，他卻不肯告訴我。

　　我不願意逼人太甚，既然他已回家，我就準備離開了，讓他好好休息一下。就在這個時候，他忽然說：「老師，你既然要知道我媽媽在哪裡工作，我現在就帶你去看。」

　　他坐上我的車子，指點我如何去，那個區域是我們做老師的人不會去的地方。最後，孩子叫我將車子停一下，指給我看他媽媽工作的地方，我一看，發現是家酒廊。我終於了解這是怎麼一回事。

　　孩子回來上課，也接受了校方的輔導。輔導室告訴我這是一個嚴重的案例，孩子雖然有一個富有的家庭，卻像一個窮苦孩子，在同學面

◇ posh [pɑʃ] (adj.) 時髦的；高尚的
◇ elevator (n.) 電梯
◇ access card 進出通行卡
◇ luxurious (adj.) 豪華的；奢侈的

◇ attest (v.) 佐證
◇ divorce (v.) 離婚
◇ attractive (adj.) 漂亮迷人的
◇ pry (v.) 刺探；打探

Sure enough, he lived in a very posh building—you couldn't get in the front door, or use the elevator, without an access card. His house was luxurious, and his new bicycle, expensive speakers and computer system attested that he was one of those kids who's got it all. His mom wasn't home when we arrived, but I'd called earlier to let her know her son had been found.

The boy told me his parents were divorced; he lived with his mother. Judging by the pictures in the house, she was very attractive. I asked if his mom worked, and he said she did, but when I asked where she worked, he wouldn't tell me.

I didn't want to pry—now that he was safe at home, I started getting ready to leave so that he could have a good rest. But then, out of the blue, he said, "Teacher, since you want to know where my mom works, I'll take you there for a look."

He got into my car and showed me the way there. We arrived in a neighborhood where teachers like me rarely set foot. Eventually he told me to pull over for a second, and he pointed to where his mom worked. I looked over and saw that it was a cocktail lounge. Finally, I understood.

The boy came back to school, where he began receiving counseling. The counselor's office told me that it was a serious case—even though the boy had a rich family, he seemed like a poor kid, unable to hold

---

◇ neighborhood (n.) 街坊
◇ eventually (adv.) 最後 (指時間)

◇ cocktail lounge 酒廊
◇ counseling (n.)（心理）輔導

前抬不起頭來，他們說孩子一定還會再出走的。

21-25　　孩子終於提出條件了，他說只要離開現在的家，他保證一定會好好地念書，不再出走了。

　　我找了社會局的社工人員，發現有一家南部教會辦的少年城肯接納他，這所少年城原來只收容家遭變故的男性青少年，我們說好說歹，他們才答應讓他去。孩子馬上答應，孩子的媽媽一開始當然不肯，可是我們向她解釋這恐怕是唯一的辦法，她也就答應了。

　　我送孩子去，在火車上，他沒有任何緊張的樣子，反而有如釋重負的感覺。他也沒有帶太多的行李，看來，他的昂貴腳踏車、電玩和音響都要成為過去式了。

　　少年城到了，當我在付計程車司機車資的時候，孩子匆匆忙忙地打開車門，向等候他的一位神父奔去，那位神父一臉驚訝，孩子奔向

◇ propose (v.) 提議
◇ compromise (n.) 折衷方案
◇ current (adj.) 目前的；現行的
◇ social worker 社會工作人員；社工
◇ church-run 教會經營的

◇ ordinarily (adv.) 一般地；平常地
◇ prevail (v.) 勸服；說動
◇ thrilled (adj.) 高興莫名的；大喜過望的；樂不可支的
◇ escort (v.) 護送

up his head in front of his classmates. They were sure he'd run away again.

Finally, the boy proposed a compromise: as long as he was allowed to leave his current home, he promised to be a good student and never run away again.　21-25

I talked to a social worker at the Department of Social Welfare and found out there was a church-run "boys' town" down south that was willing to take him. Ordinarily, they only took in boys from families that had fallen on hard times, but we eventually prevailed upon them to take the boy in. He was thrilled. Of course, his mom refused to let him go at first, but when we explained to her that it was probably the only way we could help her son, she agreed.

I escorted the boy there. During the train ride, he didn't appear nervous at all—on the contrary, it was as though he had been relieved of a heavy burden. He didn't bring too much luggage—it seemed his expensive bike, computer games and speakers were now mere relics of the past.

We arrived at the boys' town in a taxi. As I was paying the driver, the boy threw open his door and flew toward a priest who was waiting for him. He ran to the bewildered priest, embraced him and

◇ contrary (n.) 相反；相對
◇ relieved (adj.) 解除的；放心的
◇ luggage (n.) 行李
◇ relic (s) (n.) 殘留之物；遺跡
◇ bewildered (adj.) 困惑不解的；搞不清楚的

他，擁抱著他，喃喃地說：「神父，我終於回家了。」神父看清楚他以後，對他說，「原來是你！」

有一位年輕人帶他去他的房間，神父趁機告訴我，這個孩子在去年曾經來住過，他自己來的，而且也坦白地告訴神父，他有家，家也有錢，可以付生活費。他們發現他是個很好的孩子，可是既然他有家，又不窮，就勸他回去了。因為少年城是收養窮人家孩子住的地方。

26-29　我看了一下環境，又想起了孩子在台北的家，在這裡，他雖然也有一輛腳踏車，可是又破又舊，他們好多人同住一間房，這個孩子的確放棄了不少的東西。

當我離開的時候，孩子對我說：「老師，告訴我的同學我新家的地址和電話，歡迎大家到南部來看我。」說這些話的時候，孩子臉上充滿了滿足的表情。誰都可以看出他已經回家了。

在我回台北的火車上，我在想，我快結婚了，最近我看到很多有錢孩子所擁有的昂貴玩具，不覺有點擔心。以我的收入，我未來的孩子是不會有這些玩意兒的。現在我不再擔心這件事，我該隨時注意的是

◇ murmur (v.) 喃喃而語；念念有辭
◇ expenses (n.) 費用；花費（註：常使用複數形。）
◇ admonish (v.) 好言相勸
◇ purpose (n.) 宗旨；目的
◇ sacrifice (v.) 犧牲

murmured, "Father, I've finally come home." Once he got a clear look at him, the priest replied, "Oh, it was you all along!"

As a young man led the boy off to his room, the priest told me that this same boy had come to live with them a year ago. He came alone and freely admitted that he had a family, a rich family at that, and thus could pay his own expenses. They found him to be a very good boy, but since he had a home and wasn't poor, they admonished him to go back, since the purpose of the boys' town was to give children from poor families a place to live.

I took a look around, then thought again of the boy's home in Taipei. Here, although he would have a bike, it would be old and broken down; moreover, he'd have to share a bedroom with a bunch of other boys. He had indeed sacrificed a lot of material things.

26-29

As I left, the boy said to me, "Teacher, tell my classmates my new address and phone number. Tell them they're welcome to come down and see me." As he spoke, his face radiated contentment. Anyone could see that he had come home.

On the train back to Taipei, I thought about how I'd soon be getting married. Lately I'd seen a lot of expensive toys that rich children had, and I couldn't help feeling a little worried—with my income, I wouldn't be able to give my children those things. Now I no longer

◇ material things 物質享受的東西　　◇ contentment (n.) 滿足；知足
◇ radiate (v.) 散放　　◇ income (n.) 收入

我有沒有做個好人,如果我失去了孩子對我的尊敬,恐怕就失去了一切。

我終於知道了孩子們想要的是什麼樣的家。

◇ mindful(adj.)留心的;在意的

worried about that. Instead, I knew that what I ought to be mindful of was whether or not I was living a good life. If I ever lost my children's respect for me, I'd lose everything.

I finally knew what kind of home it is that a child wants.

（1）（as soon as）school gets out 學校一放學（1段）

Each day, as soon as school got out, I'd leave the campus and take a walk along a path through the countryside.

我每天一放學，就到校外去，沿著鄉間的小徑散步。

解析

「放學」兩字，看似簡單，真要用英文表達倒也不太容易。國中學過的（when）school is over 當然不成問題。在這裡，譯者告訴我們一種新的說法：（as soon as）school gets out，由此可見英文還真是很有彈性的。我曾就教譯者郝凱揚先生，「放學」可否用 when we call it a school day 和 when school closes for the day 來表示，郝先生說沒問題。也許讀者可以想想看，還有沒有別種方式來表示「放學」。

小試身手

1. 他一放學就到家附近的一家便利商店打工。

　　　　────────────────────────────

（2）run across 碰到……；遇見……（2段）

Naturally, during these walks I'd often run across children at play.

散步的時候，當然會碰到玩耍的小孩子。

解析

這是個要強勢記憶的片語，因為非母語人士很難從字面聯想到 run 和 across 的組合，會產生出「碰到」、「遇見」的意義來。介詞有「十字交叉」的意味，芸芸眾生裡，要在街上和某個熟識的人「交錯擦身」而遇，可不是容易的事，所以片語 run across 其實有「偶然相遇」、「不期而遇」的意義。介詞的使用，除了此處所見的 across，另一個選擇為 into，也就是說，也可說 run into someone 以表示和某人「偶然相遇。」

小試身手

2. 我沒想到在離婚那麼久後還會遇到她。

_____

（3）risk one's life to V（某人）冒著生命的危險……(3段)

I risked my life to pick it up for them; they were overjoyed.

我冒著生命的危險去撿了給他們，他們好高興。

解析

和上個解析重點比起來，要學會 risk one's life to V 顯得容易多了，幾乎只要見過一次，就忘也忘不了。所以我們在這裡轉個彎，還是利用 risk 這個字來考驗各位，不太有把握的讀者，可以搬救兵，而功能最好、服從性最高的，非你手邊的字典莫屬了。

小試身手

3. 當你把所有錢都投資股市時，你就冒著把所有蛋放在同一個籃子（孤注一擲）的風險。

_____

（4）（a burden）falls on one's shoulders（重擔）落在某人肩上(4段)

Then I walked by, and the burden of retrieving the ball once again fell on my shoulders.

我走過，這個撿球的工作又落到我的肩上。

解析

學過幾年英文，至少應該有個心得，即中文的某個概念，只要英文有一樣

的對應語，這個對應語就好學。這裡的解析重點即是一例，中文說「重擔」「落」「在某人肩上」，英文有百分之百的相等語，a burden ＋ falls ＋ on one's shoulders。這種英文就容易學得起來，令人遺憾的是，中英文兩者的對應關係不都是那麼契合，也因此造成學習英文的障礙和困擾。以下小試身手就多了些障礙和困擾囉。

小試身手

4.　我想甩掉落在我肩上的重擔。

　　_____

（5）文法要點：**not only** 所形成的倒裝結構（4段）

Not only did he not bark at me, he even started wagging his tail.

牠不僅沒有對我叫，反而搖起尾巴來了。

解析

Not only Aux. ＋ S. ＋ V ＋ ...

讀者們，看完以上的英譯後，你會不會覺得 Not only... 放在句子開頭的位置很奇怪呢？如果是，請你把它放回它原來該在的位置，那麼句子會呈現什麼面貌呢？如果答案是 He not only did not bark at me... 「牠不僅沒有對我叫……」那就沒錯了。

所以從上句出發，把 not only 提到句首的位置去，成為：

Not only he（did）not bark at me...（×）

不過以上的句子是錯誤的，因為英文有個規矩，即句首有 only 所形成的片語或否定詞形成的片語，跟在後面的句子主體就得使用倒裝結構。如今更不得了，not 和 only 都一起放到句首去了，倒裝結構豈可免掉呢？問題是，什麼叫作倒裝結構呢？簡單地說，就是把助動詞（Aux.）放到主詞的前面。所以

只要把上句話置於括弧內的 did 放到主詞 he 的前面去，讓句子變成（... did he not bark at me...），那就是所謂倒裝結構了。而整個句子經過這麼一番折騰，呈現出來的樣子就如以下：

Not only did he not bark at me...（○）

小試身手

5. 他不只用話罵她，而且差點對她動粗。

_____

---

(6) there is no harm in... 無害；不會怎樣；無傷大雅（6段）

Since they were so friendly to me, I figured there was no harm in asking them where they lived.

既然他們對我如此友善，我就一不做，二不休，問他們住在哪裡。

解析

雖然 harm 這個字無論作名詞或動詞都當作「傷害」解釋，此處的 there is no harm in... 在意義上卻相當於中文的「沒什麼關係」或「不會怎樣」。其實中文也有「無傷」，比如：「我問幾個私人的問題無傷吧？」這兒的「……無傷」說穿了不就是「沒什麼關係」或「不會怎樣」嗎？

小試身手

6. 我問(你)幾個私人的問題無傷吧？

_____

（7）**without a trace** 無影無蹤；一點痕跡都沒有（7段）

As soon as we set foot inside the gate, the kids scattered without a trace, off to play with the other kids.

進入了院門，孩子們溜得無影無蹤，和別的孩子們瘋去了。

解析

這是個很好學的片語，名詞 trace 的基本意義為「蹤跡」、「痕跡」，所以整個片語（without a trace）當然就是「沒有痕跡」。中文說「留下」痕跡，英文用動詞 leave 表示「留下」，以下小試身手可以利用它來發揮一下。

小試身手

7. 整個建築物就在我面前消失，沒留下一點痕跡。

　_____

（8）**come in contact with...** 接觸到（某人）（10段）

The reason was simple: all the people they came in contact with were good people.

原因很簡單，他們所接觸的人都是好人。

解析

contact 最基本的意思就是「接觸」，因此成語 come in contact with... 當然指「和……來往接觸」。除了這個成語，也可以用另一個成語 associate with... 來表達類似的意思。還有一點，讀者看得出來嗎？英譯裡的 they came in contact with 是個形容詞子句，原本的寫法是 whom they came in contact with，關係代名詞 whom 因為本身在子句裡的地位為受詞而被省略了。

注意，come in contact with 並不是那麼常用，它表示在生活中遇到的人——這些人你並不是真的跟他們交流。在以下題目中是另一個示範說明。

小試身手

8. 工作上身為一個客服代表，我遇到很多生氣的人。

_____

(9) do poorly in school 書念不好；功課不佳（10段）

If children got sick, I'd be asked to take them to see the doctor; if a child did poorly in school, I'd be asked to tutor him.

孩子病了，我被捉去開車送他們去看醫生，孩子功課不好，我又被抓去做家教。

解析

「書念不好」、「功課不佳」看似平常，用英文表達起來卻不太容易。其實你我都在非英語環境裡出生成長的，所以生活英文反倒成了問題。譯者是英文母語人士，一個 do poorly in school 隨手捻來就貼切地把「功課不好」的概念表達出來。當然這個概念的表示法不是唯一的，讀者若勤做英文閱讀，再加上常常動腦筋思考，也可以找到或自己創造出不同的表示法來。比方，do not perform well academically 或 is not a great achiever in school 或者 fall behind in his studies 也都是不錯的選項。

小試身手

9. 他們唯一的孩子功課優異，他們覺得很光榮。

_____

（10）have great respect for... 很敬重；非常尊重（10段）

Moreover, they all had great respect for us—at any given moment, we uncles and aunts could hug them, but we could also reprimand them.

不僅如此，他們也都非常尊重我們，我們這些叔叔伯伯阿姨們，隨時要抱這些孩子們，可是也都隨時可以管他們。

解析

把 have great respect for... 這個成語提出來當重點，因為它既重要而又實用。其實即使把 great 拿掉，只用 have respect for... 也很有「敬重」和「尊敬」的意思。加了 great 一字，更可以提昇「敬重」和「尊敬」的程度。除了 great 外，還可以使用一些類似的形容詞如 much, high 或 huge 等。

小試身手

10. 所有的員工對他都特別敬重，因為他是這個行業的老手。

_____

（11）submit to one's discipline 受某人管教（10段）

The kids would go to the nuns for everything, and they willingly submitted to their discipline.

他們什麼事都去找修女，也心甘情願地接受修女們的管教。

解析

submit 無論作動詞或名詞皆可作「管教」解釋。讀者們要注意的是 submit 這個動詞，它作「乖乖地接受」、「順服聽從」解釋。在英譯裡它是個不及物動詞，所以在接受詞（one's discipline）之前還要再加個介詞（to）。這種現象對初學英文的人會構成某一程度的困擾，解決之道為在碰到這類動詞時，要仔細分辨。以下的 yield「屈服」和 contribute「貢獻」就是後面常需接著介詞 to 的兩個動詞。

小試身手

11-1. 她很有說服力，所以他很快就乖乖接受她的分析。

_____

11-2. 壓力其大無比，我最後屈服其下。

_____

11-3. 他希望當他日後有錢財時能貢獻社會。

_____

(12) the vast majority of... 絕大多數的……(11段)

The students all came from middle-class homes, and the vast majority of them were perfectly normal, but there was one exception.

學生全都來自中產階級的家庭，大多數都很正常，但有一個例外。

解析

majority 本身就已經是「多數」之意，反義字為 minority，當然就是「少數」的意思。美國是個多種族的國家，除了居多數的白人、黑人、拉丁美洲人，另外還有很多人口只有幾萬或幾十萬的少數族裔，英文就以 ethnic minorities 來表示之。用 the majority of... 表示「多數的……」，再加上一個 vast 變成 the vast majority of... ，當然程度向上提升，為「絕大多數的……」的意思。

小試身手

12. 美國絕大多數的學校沒規定學生得穿制服。

_____

（13） someone's mind is/seems to be elsewhere 某人心不在焉 （11段）

This boy's mind always seemed to be elsewhere, and his schoolwork left something to be desired.

這個孩子老是有點心不在焉，功課也不太好。

解析

多數人都有分心的毛病，明明應該用心聽課，吸收老師的經驗，可以節省許多自己摸索的時間。可是實在沒辦法，要不然就想著昨晚的連續劇，要不然就捨不得桌子底下的漫畫，要不就想和隔壁哈啦兩句，這些雜事，把心思都分散掉了。上課的老師看你失魂落魄的樣子，會不會關心地奉上一句：Your mind seems to be somewhere else.

會不會有點丟臉呢？那倒也不必啦。Just put your mind back on what is going on in class.

> 小試身手
>
> 13. 老師開玩笑說：「你身在這裡，心卻在別處。」
>
> _____

（14） be perplexed as to... （某人）對（某事）困惑不解（14段）

They were perplexed as to why he would go spend the night in a train station when he lived in a building you had to swipe a card to get into.

他們完全不懂，既然他住在要刷卡才能進入的大廈裡，為什麼晚上會跑到火車站去過夜？

解析

也許對讀者而來說 perplexed 是個生字，可是讀者們對它的另一個同義字

confused 想必不會陌生，以後只要在腦海裡把兩者作個連結，就不難把 perplexed 學起來。比較要多費點心思的倒是在之後的介詞 as to，它作「對於……」或「關於……」解釋。各位國中時期學過的 about，還有 regarding 和 concerning 等字也有相似的意義與用法。

小試身手

14. 怎麼用筷子挾起一粒花生，他們一臉困惑。

_____

（15）notwithstanding... 儘管……；雖然……（15段）

Notwithstanding his great reluctance, after a great deal of effort, I finally persuaded him to let me take him home.

儘管他老大不願意，在我一再勸說以後，他答應由我陪他回家。

解析

如果告訴你，這個 notwithstanding 是介詞，你會嚇一跳嗎？當然這個字怎麼看都像現在分詞（Ving），怎麼說都不像介詞，因為介詞大多造型短小，如 in, on, at, for, with, over, under, across 之類的字。可是 notwithstanding 的確是介詞的用法，因為它之後都接著受詞，就如前一個解析重點裡所提到的 regarding 和 concerning 一樣。碰到這些字，只好投降，承認它們是介詞，一方面只好說它們是披著羊皮（分詞）的狼（介詞）了。讀者們，請再把 notwithstanding 看一眼，今天是個黃道吉日，你們碰到了一個很長的介詞。

小試身手

15. 儘管他人再三警告，他還是往池水深的那一頭過去。

_____

(16) Judging by/from... 依……論斷；憑……來研判（17段）

Judging by the pictures in the house, she was very attractive.

從家裡照片上來看，他的媽媽很漂亮。

解析

這是個固定的片語，用的是現在分詞 (Ving) 的形式，其後所接的不是 by 就是 from 這兩個介詞其中的一個。使用 from，當然和 from 的字面意義相吻合，為「從……研判」；若使用 by，則比較傾向「根據……來判斷」的意思。

小試身手

16. 從她一臉困惑(的表情)來看，我知道她一點都不可能幫上我什麼忙。

_____

(17) set foot 涉足（19段）

We arrived in a neighborhood where teachers like me rarely set foot.

那個區域是我們做老師的人不會去的地方。

解析

讀者不覺得 set 和 foot 這兩個字的組合 (set foot) 很讓人有「踩」或「踏」的感覺嗎？嫦娥和吳剛兩個有待考證的中國人不算，第一個「踏」上月球的人是誰呢？某人和你大吵一架，此後打死不肯「踏」進你家一步。以上兩個例子，都很適合使用 set foot 來表達「踏」這個字的意思。

小試身手

17-1. 我發誓絕不再踏進那家商店。

_____

17-2. 第一個踏上月球的人是誰呢？

_____

17-3. 他打死不肯踏進我家一步。

_____

（18）**as long as...** 只要……（21段）

Finally, the boy proposed a compromise: as long as he was allowed to leave his current home, he promised to be a good student and never run away again.

孩子終於提出條件了，他說只要離開現在的家，他保證一定會好好地念書，不再出走了。

解析

讀者們要注意一點，這個 as long as 為連接詞，後面接著主詞和動詞，形成一個副詞子句。以上是理論，我們不妨把它和實務結合起來。中文說：「只要提供他充份的資源……」，這句話裡的「只要提供他充份的資源」，是一種**副詞子句**，更精確地說叫作**條件副詞子句**，而這個「只要」的英文為 as long as，也可以用 so long as，它們都是連接詞，後面繼續接主詞「他」（he），「被提供」（is provided），整個子句完成之後如下：as long as he is provided with sufficient resources。

讀者要特別留意，以上只是一個副詞子句，它還要搭配一個主要子句，整個「句子」才算大功告成。而主要子句就是「只要提供他充份的資源……」裡，那個「……」的部份。如果讓你接續寫下去，你會填入哪些字，來造就一個主要子句呢？以下小試身手幫你做了示範（即把「……」的部份完成），但更歡迎你花點時間，用點腦力 DIY。

小試身手

18. 只要提供他充份的資源，他就一定能克服那個困難。

_____

（19）fall on hard times 家道中落；家庭遭到變故（22段）

Ordinarily, they only took in boys from families that had fallen on hard times, but we eventually prevailed upon them to take the boy in.

這所少年城原來只收容家遭變故的男性青少年，我們說好說歹，他們才答應讓他去。

解析

hard times 大致上很趨近「時機不好」、「時局不佳」。處在這種情況，有些家庭在這種苦境的漩渦裡無法度過難關，逆境的打擊一來，往往應聲而倒（fall），家道就此旁落。所以 fall on hard times 很適合解釋成「家道旁落」或「家運因時機不佳而中衰」。

小試身手

19. 那個家庭家道中衰過好幾次，而每次都能重新站起。

_____

（20）be relieved of（a burden）去掉負擔；卸下重荷（23段）

During the train ride, he didn't appear nervous at all—on the contrary, it was as though he had been relieved of a heavy burden.

在火車上，他沒有任何緊張的樣子，反而有如釋重負的感覺。

解析

先從主動說起吧。主動語態的片語原是這個樣子的：relieve someone of something。比如：「他們解除了我的責任。」英文的說法是：They relieved me of my duties. 把主動的 relieve someone of something 化為被動，則形式為 someone is relieved of something。以前例言，中文即為：「我被（他們）解除了職務。」以英文言，則為：I was relieved of my duties.

小試身手

20. 他沒對我說：「你被開除了，」而是說：「你職務被解除了。」

_____

（21）It was you all along! 原來是你！（24段）

Once he got a clear look at him, the priest replied, "Oh, it was you all along!"

神父看清楚他以後，對他說，「原來是你！」

解析

只看 it was you 三個字，不難知道意思為「是你」。如今後面再加 all along 兩個字，加進了「一直都是」、「一路走來」的意思，更讓人深切感受到口語英文的味道。例如：I have loved you all along.（我一直都愛著你。）

小試身手

21. 喔，原來是你出錢讓我一路讀完大學的。

_____

（22）be mindful of... 留心……；注意……（28段）

Instead, I knew that what I ought to be mindful of was whether or not I was living a good life.

（現在我不再擔心這件事，）我該隨時注意的是我有沒有做個好人。

解析

英譯裡，除了 be mindful of... 這個片語之外，還有幾個值得一學的東西。第一個是位置在句首的 instead，表示和之前語意相逆的轉折，相當於中文「反而」這方面的意思。比如中文說：「你不應該嘲笑他們。反而，你要盡力幫助他們。」英文可以這麼寫：Instead of laughing at them, you should do what you can to help them.

另外讀者還可以看到分別作主詞和主詞補語的兩個名詞子句。作主詞的名詞子句為：what I ought to be mindful of；而作主詞補語的名詞子句為：whether or not I was living a good life。

這個和文法有關的觀念很繁雜嗎？其實不然，請繼續往下看：

句型：S. + V. + S.C.

用名詞作主詞和主詞補語：S. → 老虎 (tigers)；S.C. → 瀕臨絕種的動物 (endangered species)

句子：老虎是瀕臨絕種的動物。

S. + V. + S.C. → Tigers are endangered species.

用**名詞子句**作主詞和主詞補語：S. → 我所正在思考的事情（what I am thinking about）；S.C. → 我該邀請誰來參加宴會（who I should invite to the party）

句子：我所正在思考的事情是我該邀請誰來參加宴會。

S. + V. + S.C. → What I am thinking about is who I should invite to the party.

小試身手

22. 他要我留心在事情過後會有什麼後續（發展）。

_____

小試身手解答

1. He goes to work at a convenience store near his house as soon as school gets out.

2. I never imagined I would run into her again so long after the divorce.

3. You run the risk of putting all your eggs in one basket when you invest all your money in the stock market.

4. I tried to shake off the burden which fell on my shoulders.

5. Not only did he abuse her verbally, but he almost got physical with her.

6. There is no harm in my asking (you) a few personal questions, is there?

7. The whole building just disappeared in front of me without leaving a trace.

8. In my job as a customer service representative, I come in contact with a lot of angry people.

9. They are proud that their only child does exceptionally well in school.

10. All the employees have a special respect for him because he is a veteran in the trade.

11-1. She was very persuasive, and he quickly submitted to her reasoning.

11-2. The pressure was so overwhelming that I yielded to it at last.

11-3. He hoped to contribute to society when he had the means to do so someday.

12. The vast majority of American schools do not require students to wear uniforms.

13. "Your body is here but your mind is elsewhere," joked the teacher.

14. They looked perplexed as to how to pick up a peanut with a pair of chopsticks.

15. Notwithstanding repeated warnings from the others, he ventured towards the deep end of the pool.

16. Judging by her confused look, I knew she was the last person in the world who could help me.

17-1. I swear I will never set foot in that store again.

17-2. Who was the first man to set foot on the moon?

17-3. He utterly refused to set foot in my house.

18. As long as he is provided with sufficient resources, he is sure to overcome the difficulty.

19. The family fell on hard times on several occasions, but each time it rose to its feet again.

20. Instead of saying, "You're fired," he said to me, "You've been relieved of your duties."

21. Oh, it was you all along who supported me through college.

22. He told me to be mindful of what would follow after the event.

The Eavesdroppers
竊聽者

1-5　　　我的專長是遙控技術，工作地點是美國的一家專門設計通訊衛星的公司，在過去，衛星放上去以後，要修起來是很困難的事，可是我們現在的做法是事先將衛星裡面設計好了可以遙控的維修系統，如果衛星失靈，我們可以在地面送一些訊號上去，也可以因此找出毛病的問題所在，如果情形不嚴重，我們可以在地面用遙控的方法將它修好。

　　衛星很少失靈，我們平時就做一些遙控的檢驗工作，這些檢驗做多了，大家也就馬馬虎虎，只要功能正常，我們一概都在數據上簽字了事。

　　一個月以前，我閒來無事，將檢驗的數據仔細看看，忽然發現了一個怪異的現象，這個現象過去沒有的，兩年前才開始有，因為不正常的程度非常之小，不影響運作，所以沒有人發現。

　　我立刻向我的上司報告這件事，他調出了好幾顆衛星的資料，這才發現，兩年前，大家都正常，現在都有問題了。

CD2-6
◇ expert（n.）專家
◇ remote control（n.）遙控（此處指遙控技術，但也可指家用電器的遙控器。）
◇ technology（n.）科技
◇ specialize（v.）擅長；專精
◇ communication satellite（n.）通訊衛星
◇ install（v.）安裝；裝設
◇ malfunction（v.）故障
◇ signal（n.）信（訊）號
◇ perfunctory（adj.）隨便的；草率的；敷衍的
◇ properly（adv.）正常地

1-5
CD2-5

I'm an expert on remote control technology, and I work at an American company that specializes in designing communication satellites. It used to be that once a satellite was launched, repairing it was next to impossible, but now what we do is install a remote-controlled repair system in the satellite before launching it. Then, if the satellite malfunctions, we can send up some signals to find what caused the malfunction to occur, and if it isn't serious, we can fix it from earth by remote control.

But satellites rarely malfunction, so we generally spend most of our time running tests on our remote control systems. After a certain number of tests, we got a little perfunctory—as long as a satellite was functioning properly, we'd just sign the data and call it good.

Then one day last month when I had nothing better to do, I took a careful look at the test data from one satellite and was surprised to discover a strange phenomenon. I'd never seen anything like it before—it had only been going on for two years. Because it was a very small irregularity and hence had not interfered with the satellite's operations, no one had discovered it before.

I immediately reported the news to my boss. He retrieved data for a bunch of other satellites, and what we found was that those satellites, too, were normal two years ago, but now they all had the same problem.

◇ phenomenon (n.) 現象
◇ irregularity (n.) 不正常；異常
◇ interfere (with) (v.) 干涉；影響
◇ operation (s) (n.) 運作

◇ boss (n.) 老闆；上司；上級
◇ retrieve (v.) 取回；(重新)找回
◇ normal (adj.) 正常的

我們有一個備而不用的緊急掃描系統，通常這是在衛星有問題時才啟動的，我的上司決定啟動這種系統，結果令我們嚇得一身冷汗，原來有人在我們的衛星上裝了竊聽器，而且竊聽器的天線一概朝向太空。

6-10 　事情鬧大了，連美國總統都知道了，他立刻經由國務院和幾個超級強國聯絡，請他們查看一下，他們的衛星有沒有被竊聽。回信是：幾乎全部都已被竊聽，而且天線都朝向太空。

　聯合國安理會五強秘密地開會，一致決定在美國馬利蘭州的太空總署設立一個小組，選定一個熱線頻道，用這個頻道，告訴地球以外的外星人，我們已知道自己被竊聽，也願意和他們聯絡。五國都派出一些科學家和語言學家，到太空總署去待命。

　我是始作俑者，當然也就被派去，我們整整等一個星期，總算還好，終於有訊號回來了，文字是法文，好在我們有專家在場，立刻將之譯成英文。

◇ activate（v.）啟動
◇ emergency scanning system（n.）緊急掃描系統
◇ situation（n.）情形；狀況
◇ bug（v.）竊聽（註：尤指暗地安裝器材所進行的竊聽。）
◇ bugging device（s）（n.）竊聽裝置
◇ the Department of State 國務院（為美國政府組織裡的聯邦行政最高權力部門，相當於行政院，主持人叫作國務卿。）
◇ superpower（n.）超級強國；強權
◇ antenna（n.）天線
◇ five permanent members of the UN Security Council 聯合國安全理事會五個常任理事國

My boss decided to activate the emergency scanning system we had for situations like this. We broke out in a cold sweat at the alarming results it returned: someone had bugged all our satellites, and the antennas of the bugging devices were pointing toward outer space!

The news traveled fast; soon the American president found out. He immediately got in touch with the Department of State and several superpowers and told them to check whether their satellites were being bugged as well. Their reply: nearly all of them were, and the antennas of the bugging devices were pointing toward outer space.

6-10

The five permanent members of the UN Security Council convened a secret meeting. They adopted a unanimous resolution to assemble a team at NASA in Maryland, select a communication frequency, and transmit a message to the extraterrestrials telling them we knew we were being bugged and we were willing to speak with them. Each of the five nations sent scientists and linguists to NASA to await orders.

Of course, being the one responsible for this mess, I was sent there too. After an entire week of waiting, to our great relief we finally picked up a return signal. It was in French, but fortunately we had expert interpreters on hand who provided an immediate English translation.

◇ convene (v.) 召集；召開 (會議)
◇ unanimous [juˋnænəməs] (adj.) 全體一致的
◇ resolution (n.) 決議
◇ assemble (v.) 組合；組成
◇ NASA 美國國家航空太空總署 (全名為 National Aeronautics and Space Administration)
◇ transmit (v.) 傳輸；傳送
◇ extraterrestrial (n.) 外星人
◇ linguist (n.) 語言學家
◇ return signal (n.) 回傳的訊 (信) 號
◇ interpreter [ɪnˋtɝprɪtɚ] (n.) 傳譯者；口譯員

外星人說他們是宇宙生物研究員,因為所居住的星球離地球很遠,地球所送出去的電訊要兩個月才會到他們那裡。碰巧他出來開會,太空船路過地球,收到了訊號,也就在太空船上和我們通訊。

他說他對竊聽感到很抱歉,他只想收集資料而已,絕無任何惡意。

11-15　因為來文是法文,我們公推一位法國籍的科學家和這位外星人談話。他首先問這位外星人的專長是什麼?外星人告訴我們,他是宇宙生物研究院動物研究所的研究員,他的專長是動物的社會行為。

法國人問他為什麼要竊聽我們人類的廣播?外星人說人類是動物中的一種,他一直研究人類的社會行為。過去他們常派太空船來地球搜集有關人類的資料,現在由於人類使用通訊衛星,他們就決定在這些通訊衛星上都裝了竊聽器,所有人類的廣播都送到了他們的電腦。這樣,他們可以充分地了解人類最近所發生的事情,因此,他們研究的材料就豐富多了。

◇ alien (n.) 外地人;外星人
◇ colleague (n.) 同事
◇ transmission (n.) (指訊息) 傳輸;傳遞
◇ fortuitous (adj.) 偶然的;意外的
◇ conference (n.) 大會;(尤指許多代表參與的) 會議
◇ apologize (v.) 道歉
◇ eavesdrop [ˈivzˌdrɑp] (v.) 偷聽;竊聽
◇ incoming (adj.) 進來的;內傳的
◇ appoint (v.) 任命;指派
◇ expertise (n.) 專業知識
◇ social behavior 社會行為

The alien said that he and his colleagues were universal biology researchers. Because their home planet was a great distance away from earth, transmissions from earth normally took two months to reach them. By a fortuitous coincidence, however, they picked up our signal as they were passing by earth on their way to a conference, so they were able to communicate with us directly from their ship.

He apologized for eavesdropping on us, but said they were only gathering information—they meant no harm.

Because the incoming signal was in French, we appointed a French scientist to speak with the alien. The first thing he asked was what the alien's area of expertise was. The alien said he was a researcher from the zoology department of the Universal Academy of Biology specializing in the social behavior of animals. 11-15

The Frenchman asked him why he was eavesdropping on our broadcasts. The alien explained that humans were a type of animal, and his research had always focused on the social behavior of humans. They used to send spaceships to earth to gather data on us, but now that we used communication satellites, they had decided to bug our satellites instead: that way, all our broadcasts would go straight into their computers. With this greater abundance of research materials, they were able to gain a more comprehensive understanding of recent human affairs.

◇ broadcast(s) (n.)廣播
◇ research materials 研究資料　　　◇ comprehensive (adj.)廣泛的；全面的

　　他再一次強調竊聽的目的是為了做研究，沒有任何其他的目的，請我們一定要放心。

　　法國人問他為何對人類的社會行為有如此大的興趣？外星人說人類雖然是動物中的一種，可是人類有一個特點，那就是人類會大規模自相殘殺。他說，以獅子和老虎為例，獅子和老虎都會殺害別的動物，可是絕不殺同類，你從來沒有看過獅子吃獅子，換句話說，獅子和老虎會認出自己的同類來，而盡量避免殺自己的同類。

　　外星人還說人類自相殘殺，常常好像為一些奇怪而令他們不解的理由，以宗教為例，宗教都是勸人為善，更都規勸信仰宗教者要愛人，可是人類卻一再地為宗教而互相殺戮。

16-20　　再以奧克拉荷馬城的爆炸案來講，嫌疑犯和被殺的人屬於同一種族，信仰同一宗教，而仍然會大開殺戒，令外星人大惑不解。

　　外星人對人類會以酷刑來對待同胞，也表示不了解，他說貓有時會

◇ ulterior (adj.) 外部的；外在的
◇ motive (n.) 動機
◇ unique (adj.) 獨具的；獨特的
◇ characteristic (adj.) 特色；特徵
◇ scale (n.) 規模
◇ recognize (v.) 認得；辨識
◇ incomprehensible (adj.) 無法理解的；難懂的
◇ admonish (v.) 好言相勸
◇ pretext (n.) 藉口；託辭

Again, he emphasized that the eavesdropping was for research purposes only—they had no ulterior motives. He urged us not to worry.

The Frenchman asked why he was so interested in human social behavior. The alien replied that despite being a type of animal, humans have a very unique characteristic: they kill each other on a large scale. He pointed out how lions and tigers, for example, will kill other animals but never their own kind. No one has ever seen a lion eating a lion—in other words, lions and tigers recognize their own kind.

He also said that people often kill each other for strange reasons incomprehensible to him and his fellow aliens. For instance, take religion—all religions teach people to do good and admonish them to love others, but humans have used religion as a pretext for slaughtering each other on numerous occasions.

To take another example, the suspects in the Oklahoma City bombing were the same race as their victims, and they believed in the same religion, but they murdered them all anyway. The alien and his colleagues were utterly bewildered by this. **16-20**

He further expressed confusion at the way humans brutally torture

---

◇ slaughter (v.) 屠殺
◇ numerous (adj.) 眾多的
◇ suspect (n.) 嫌犯
◇ victim (n.) 遇害者；罹難者

◇ utterly (adv.) 完全地
◇ bewildered (adj.) 困惑的；不解的
◇ brutally (adv.) 殘暴地；殘忍地
◇ torture (v.) 對……用刑；拷打

虐待老鼠，可是從來沒有看到貓虐待其他貓的。他說他們有各種人類酷刑的錄影帶，看過的研究員都被人類的殘忍嚇壞了。

　　外星人接著說，人類中的白人看到黑人，有時會將他們不當人類看，可是動物反而不會，以豹子為例，豹子中有黑豹，也有金錢豹，可是豹子們互相都能認出，不管黑豹也好，金錢豹也好，都是豹子，貓狗也是如此，從沒有聽說黑貓攻擊白貓的，為什麼人類始終如此在意對方的膚色，這點也使他大惑不解。

　　外星人滔滔不絕的言論，使我們整個大廳鴉雀無聲，每個人都對著自己的終端機發呆，一陣沉寂以後，那位法國科學家又問外星人要到哪裡去。

　　外星人說他們正要到一個星球去開會，這個宇宙會議專門討論人類的社會行為，自從人類使用原子彈以後，研究人類的社會行為就成了宇宙學術界的顯學，過一陣子，就會有舉行會議討論這個問題。由於

◇ abuse（v.）凌虐；粗暴對待
◇ video（n.）影片（尤指錄製於錄影帶或光碟片上者）
◇ method（n.）方法
◇ terrified（adj.）驚嚇的；害怕的
◇ cruelty（n.）殘忍；殘暴
◇ exhibit（v.）表現；顯現
◇ panther（n.）豹（尤其指黑豹，或單一顏色的豹，如頑皮豹卡通裡的那位主角）
◇ leopard ['lɛpəd]（n.）豹（尤指花豹）
◇ appearance（n.）外觀；外表；外貌
◇ analysis（n.）分析

one another. He pointed out how cats will sometimes abuse mice, but they never abuse other cats. He said that they had videos of all kinds of methods of torture used among us, and the researchers who watched them were terrified by our cruelty.

The alien went on to say that when white people looked at black people, some of them didn't even consider them people at all, but animals exhibited no such behavior. For example, in the genus Panthera, there are black panthers and there are leopards, but despite their different appearances, they recognize each other as the same kind of cat. Dogs and cats are the same way—no one's ever heard of black cats attacking white cats. So why do humans care so much about skin color? He and his colleagues were at a loss to explain.

As the alien's stream of analysis flowed on and on, a hush fell over the room. Everyone stared blankly at his computer terminal. After a long, heavy silence, the French scientist asked the alien where he was headed.

The alien said he and his crewmates were on their way to a certain planet to attend a universe-wide conference on human social behavior. Ever since humans started using atomic bombs, human social behavior had become a hot research topic in universal academic circles, which was why the conference was being held to discuss it.

◇ hush (n.) 靜默；靜肅
◇ blankly (adv.) 茫然地
◇ computer terminal 電腦終端機
◇ (be) headed 前往 (某地)
◇ crewmate (n.) (同機；同船；同一載具的) 同僚或夥伴
◇ atomic bomb (n.) 原子彈
◇ academic circle 學術界；學術圈

他是此方面的權威，所以也就常被請去發表論文。

21-25　最後，法國人和我們大家商量以後，大膽地提出的一個問題，他問，對外星人而言，「人類」的學名是什麼。

外星人說了一個名字，是音譯，沒有人懂。所以法國人問他這個學名的意義何在。

外星人說這個學名的意義是「進化尚未完成」，他說人類是比較晚出來的一種動物，因此，進化可能尚未完成，所以才會有如此自相殘殺的行為，他的理論是，只要假以時日，人類也會像其他動物一樣，不再有戰爭，也不再虐待自己的同類。

然後他說他一定要走了，希望將來有一天有互相面對面的機會。

當天晚上，在我看新聞的時候，又看到盧安達另一次大屠殺的畫面，讓我想起外星人的話，卻也想起我小學的時候就學會的一句話，「人是萬物之靈」，這句話對嗎？

26　我仍希望這句話是對的。

◇ authority (n.) 權威人士
◇ consult (v.) 會商；討論
◇ boldly (adv.) 大膽地
◇ transliteration (n.) 直譯 (如將「好久不見」譯為 Long time no see.)
◇ evolve (v.) 進化；演化

Because he was an authority on the subject, he had been invited to speak.

Finally, after consulting with us, the French scientist boldly asked the aliens what they had chosen as their scientific name for humans. **21-25**

The alien gave a transliteration of the name, which no one understood. So the Frenchman asked what the name meant.

The alien said it meant "not yet fully evolved". He said humans were a relatively late-emerging animal, so it was possible that their evolution was still incomplete, which would explain why they killed each other so much. His theory was that given enough time, humans would eventually become like other animals: they would cease fighting wars and stop abusing their own kind.

Then he said he had to say goodbye, but he hoped we would have the chance to meet face to face someday.

That night, as I was reading the news, I saw another picture of the carnage in Rwanda. It reminded me of what the alien had said, and it also made me think of a quote I had learned in elementary school: "Man is the soul of the universe." Was that really true?

I still hoped it was true. **26**

◇ emerge (v.) 出現　　　　　　　　◇ carnage (n.) 屠殺；濫殺
◇ incomplete (adj.) 不完整的；不完全的　　◇ quote (n.) 名言；引言
◇ cease (v.) 停止

（1）（be）an expert on... 精通……；擅長……；為……的專家（1段）

I'm an expert on remote control technology, and I work at an American company that specializes in designing communication satellites.

我的專長是遙控技術，工作地點是美國的一家專門設計通訊衛星的公司。

解析

expert 一般作名詞居多，以上的英譯句中的即是，它的意思為「專家」、「學有專精的人」，其後常接 on 這個介詞，之後再接著精通擅長的領域。比如你想以英文表達「他是位談判專家／高手。」即可用（He's an expert on negotiation.）來表現。在此要特別提醒讀者，expert 也可以作形容詞解，意思為「專精的」、「內行的」，要注意的是此時，其後常使用 at 這個介詞。在此情況下，前面相同的那句話：「他是位談判專家／高手。」可以寫為（He's expert at negotiating.）

> 小試身手
>
> 1. 全世界的污染控制專家都被徵召而來。
>
> ＿＿＿＿＿＿＿＿＿＿＿＿＿＿＿＿＿＿＿＿＿＿

（2）next to impossible 幾近不可能（1段）

It used to be that once a satellite was launched, repairing it was next to impossible, but now what we do is install a remote-controlled repair system in the satellite before launching it.

在過去，衛星放上去以後，要修起來是很困難的事，可是我們現在的做法是事先將衛星裡面設計好了可以遙控的維修系統。

解析

不妨就這麼來學這個片語了。你到國家音樂廳看表演，中場休息時候，燈光打亮，你往身旁一看，不得了，美國前總統就坐在你身邊 (The former president of the United States is sitting right next to you.)，難怪你從一開始就有一種莫名的安全感。

看到沒，next to... 原本指的是「在……旁邊」，也就是「很接近……」、「很靠近……」的意思。既然如此，next to impossible 不就是「很接近不可能」，也就是中文常說的「幾近不可能」的意思嗎？

小試身手

2. 一個人要以一天時間從台北騎單車至高雄幾乎是不可能的事。

_____

（3）run a test on... 對……進行測試（2段）

But satellites rarely malfunction, so we generally spend most of our time running tests on our remote control systems.
衛星很少失靈，我們平時就做一些遙控的檢驗工作。

解析

整個 run a test on... 片語所使用的四個字裡，動詞 run 的用法最令人費解。但發揮一些想像力，仔細思量後，讀者也應該覺得好玩。看過人們在運動場上跑步健身嗎？沿著跑道，一圈一圈地跑 (run)，一旁看的人覺得無趣，慢跑的人卻樂在其中。

讀者們請回到主題來，就是 run 這個字。它給我們的意象是從起點到終點，週而復始，不停地「跑」(run)。所以，假如檢測工作 (test) 就像跑道，是個有開頭有結束的程序，那麼用 run a test 以表達「進行一套檢測程序」不也有趣而合理嗎？

小試身手

3. 他們決定在銷售軟體之前先進行更多測試。

_____

（4）have nothing better to do 閒來沒事；閒著沒事（3段）

Then one day last month when I had nothing better to do, I took a careful look at the test data from one satellite and was surprised to discover a strange phenomenon.

一個月以前，我閒來無事，將檢驗的數據仔細看看，忽然發現了一個怪異的現象。

解析

使用 have nothing better to do 這個用語來表現「閒來沒事」實在譯得很妙。從字面上來看，它是「找不到更好的事情做」的意思。你在家裡晃來晃去，無所事事，家裡的老母看不過去，是否跟你說過：「如果你閒著沒事，去把碗盤洗一洗。」在老母眼裡，洗碗不是什麼舒服愉快的事情，但總比「找不到更好的事情做」好。

如果你現在就閒閒沒事，就讓我們把老母的話當成題目練習吧。Give it a try if you have nothing better to do at the moment.

小試身手

4-1. 如果你閒著沒事，去把碗盤洗一洗。

_____

4-2. 閒著沒事，我把電腦開機開始玩一些遊戲，只是打發時間。

_____

（5）break out in a cold sweat 嚇出一身冷汗；冒一身冷汗（5段）

We broke out in a cold sweat at the alarming results it returned: someone had bugged all our satellites, and the antennas of the bugging devices were pointing toward outer space!

結果令我們嚇得一身冷汗，原來有人在我們的衛星上裝了竊聽器，而且天線一概朝向太空。

解析

很活潑的一個片語，和中文的「嚇出 (break out) 一身冷汗 (in a cold sweat)」百分之百吻合。其實 break out 豈止這樣的用法，break out with chicken pox 長出水痘；break out of jail 逃出監獄；break out the champagne 拿出香檳，以你的想像，思考一下為什麼這些狀況都用了 break 一字。

小試身手

5. 沉重的腳步聲愈來愈近時，我嚇出一身冷汗。

_____

（6）pick up（a signal）接收到（信號）（8段）

After an entire week of waiting, to our great relief we finally picked up a return signal.

我們整整等一個星期，總算還好，終於有訊號回來了。

解析

請特別注意，片語 pick up 除了習見的「（以車）接（某人）」意思，還有「（學）得」和「接收」這方面的意思。這次我們把 pick up 的這三個基本用法都放在小試身手裡。

小試身手

6-1. 她說她希望車子到哪裡接她？

_____

6-2. 我待在阿根廷那段期間學了一些西班牙文。

_____

6-3. 我當時在偏遠的山區裡，行動電話接收不到任何訊號。

_____

(7)（be）a great distance（away）from... 距⋯⋯很遙遠（9段）

Because their home planet was a great distance away from earth,
transmissions from earth normally took two months to reach them.

因為所居住的星球離地球很遠，地球所送出去的電訊要兩個月才會到他
們那裡。

解析

所以大家學到了，某地或某物距離你很遠，可以使用（be）a great
distance（away）from... 來表達。請各位舉一反二，進一步想想看，若要表達
「某地或某物距離你很近」又該怎麼說呢？有時候，既不講近，也不講遠，
而只想要表達「在某個適切的距離」，又該如何呢？我們還是把這三個用法
都放在小試身手裡，讓讀者們從實做中學習。

7-1. 我常常旅行到離家很遠的地方。

_____

7-2. 現代噴射客機的出現，使得從紐約飛到洛杉磯變成是很近的距離
　　（變得很近）。

_____

7-3. 這幅圖在某個距離最能充份欣賞出來（最好看）。

_____

(8) eavesdrop on... 偷聽……；竊聽……（10段）

He apologized for eavesdropping on us, but said they were only
gathering information—they meant no harm.
他說他對竊聽感到很抱歉，他只想收集資料而已，絕無任何惡意。

解析

像間諜（spy）一樣「尾隨監視」目標的一舉一動，英文有個片語 spy on... 可
以表示。說到這裡，讀者們應該更容易理解，為什麼 eavesdrop on... 是「偷
／竊聽……」，也更容易學會它了。以下的練習，該用哪一個呢？

8.　這顆衛星要被發射升空來監視敵人的軍事活動。

_____

(9) focus on... 重點擺在……；以……為主（12段）

The alien explained that humans were a type of animal, and his research had always focused on the social behavior of humans.

外星人說人類是動物中的一種，他一直研究人類的社會行為。

解析

focus 作名詞時為「焦點」，是個光學上的名詞。在片語 focus on... 裡，它是動詞，作「聚焦」，即把光線集中到某一個點（即焦點）。引申到各種不同的情境裡，就成了「把……集中在（某處，某物）」的意思。比如，我們可以把「注意力」集中在某事（物），可以把「興趣」集中在某事（物），可以把「精力」集中在某事（物）。有沒有道理？

> 小試身手
>
> 9. 他把自己關進實驗室，把所有時間和精力集中以求發現那種神祕物質。
>
> _____

(10) gain a more comprehensive understanding of... 對……有更廣泛的了解（12段）

With this greater abundance of research materials, they were able to gain a more comprehensive understanding of recent human affairs.

這樣，他們可以充分的了解人類最近所發生的事情，因此，他們研究的材料就豐富多了。

解析

動詞 gain 作「得到」、「達到」解。因此基本片語 gain an understanding of... 就表達了「對……有所了解」的意思。其實片語 gain a more comprehensive understanding of... 可以改寫為 understand... more comprehensively，兩者

的意思一樣。無論是形容詞 comprehensive 或者是副詞 comprehensively，兩者都表達「廣泛」、「通盤」的意思。因此，gain a more comprehensive understanding of... 和 understand... more comprehensively 兩者都表示「對……有更廣泛、更通盤的了解」。

英譯裡另外有兩個值得讀者一學的東西：this greater abundance of 和 research materials。前者由片語 a great abundance of 而來，意思是「大量的」、「豐盛的」，後者則是「研究資料」之意。

小試身手

10. 我知道我得做進一步的研究才能對那個現象有更深入的了解。

_____

---

(11) for research purpose only 只為了研究的目的／用途（13段）

Again, he emphasized that the eavesdropping was for research purposes only—they had no ulterior motives.

他再一次強調竊聽的目的是為了做研究，沒有任何其他的目的。

解析

有一部 007 電影，中文譯名為「最高機密」，英文原片名呢？哦，它就叫作 For Your Eyes Only。就只讓你的眼睛過目，其他任何記錄都不可以留下。這不叫作最高機密，還能是什麼呢？因此，讀者看到這裡的 for research purpose only，馬上就可以反應得過來，這個用語指的是「純粹只供研究的用途，沒有其他的目的。」

小試身手

11. 以下所列答案僅供參考之用。

_____

（12）despite Ving... 儘管……（14段）

The alien replied that despite being a type of animal, humans have a very unique characteristic: they kill each other on a large scale.

外星人說人類雖然是動物中的一種，可是人類有一個特點，那就是人類會大規模自相殘殺。

解析

儘管在前幾輯裡曾介紹過介詞 despite 的用法，但是因為它太重要了，而且多數學習者很容易疏忽它的詞性和用法，所以在此處仍然把它提出來，重新介紹一遍。讀者們，請記住了，despite 和你所熟悉的 at, for, by, against, about 之類的字一樣，叫作介詞，意義為「儘管」、「雖然」。基本上 despite 後面是要接名詞的，但是如果不湊巧，後面跟著「動詞」，那麼無論如何你也要把這個動詞字尾添個（-ing），把它「名詞」化，即是所謂的是「動名詞」。

為了讓以上的解說更具體，請看以下的例子：

（一）他因為毀損破壞公物而被判有罪。He was found guilty of vandalism.

（二）他因為販售違禁藥品被判有罪。He was found guilty of selling illegal drugs.

讀者可觀察到了，句（一）裡的介詞後面跟著「名詞」，即（vandalism）；而句（二）同樣的介詞後面跟的是「動名詞」，即（selling）。

最後，請讀者不要把它和另一個常見、意義也是「雖然」的字（although）兩者用法相混淆。although 的身份是連接詞，它和 if, when, because 等字一樣，後面要接著子句。請看以下，這些連接詞所引導的子句都已經幫你打點妥當，未完成（即主要子句）的部份（即劃線的部份）讀者可以自己來。

（三）　如果我們在這裡種棵蘋果樹，……

　　　If we plant an apple tree here, _____

（四）我下週三到新加坡時，……

When I go to Singapore next Wednesday, ＿＿＿＿＿＿＿＿＿＿

（五）因為天氣很熱，……

Because it is extremely hot, ＿＿＿＿＿＿＿＿＿＿＿＿

（六）雖然我歌唱得不好，……

Although I'm not a good singer, ＿＿＿＿＿＿＿＿＿＿＿

小試身手

12. 雖然對她有信心，但我仍不免擔心。

＿＿＿＿＿＿＿＿＿＿＿＿＿＿＿＿＿＿＿＿

（13）（be）incomprehensible to someone 無法為某人所理解（15段）

He also said that people often kill each other for strange reasons incomprehensible to him and his fellow aliens.

外星人還說人類自相殘殺，常常好像為一些奇怪而令他們不解的理由。

解析

中間的 incomprehensible 當然是整個片語的關鍵字。它的意思是「難懂的」、「無法理解領會的」。請記住，介詞用的是 to 這個字。

小試身手

13. 即使在今天，相對論仍然無法為大部份人所理解。

＿＿＿＿＿＿＿＿＿＿＿＿＿＿＿＿＿＿＿＿

（14）as a pretext for... 當作……的託辭（15段）

For instance, take religion—all religions teach people to do good and admonish them to love others, but humans have used religion as a pretext for slaughtering each other on numerous occasions.

以宗教為例，宗教都是勸人為善，更都規勸信仰宗教者要愛人，可是人類卻一再地為宗教而互相殺戮。

解析

pretext 為名詞，作「藉口」、「託辭」解釋。因此，as a pretext 為「當作藉口」、「作為託辭」之意，而 as a pretext for Ving 也就成了「當成（做某事的）藉口」、「作為（做某事的）託辭」的意思。譯者很巧妙地運用意譯的技巧，用 used religion as a pretext for slaughtering each other on numerous occasions 來詮釋「為宗教而互相殺戮」，傳達了「把宗教當成幌子而互相殺戮」這樣的意思。

小試身手

14. 示威者指控國際世貿組織用促進自由貿易的名義來剝削窮人。

_____

（15）（further）express confusion at... （進一步）表達對……的不解（17段）

He further expressed confusion at the way humans brutally torture one another.

外星人對人類會以酷刑來對待同胞，也表示不了解。

解析

名詞 confusion 的原意為「困惑」，所以片語 express confusion at... 的意思為「對……表示困惑不解」。在這個片語之前加一個副詞 further，是為了表

示「更進一步」，因而整個 further express confusion at... 就表示著「更進一步對……表示困惑不解」。confusion 的形容詞為 confused，讀者們可能對它更為熟悉，之後所接的介詞除了用 at，使用 by 或 about 也很常見。比如：I was confused by the strange ways he acted and talked.

> **小試身手**
>
> 15. 對於他們編列預算和花費的方式／過程，他更表示不解。
>
> _____

（16）be at a loss to V... 不知道該怎麼……（18段）

So why do humans care so much about skin color? He and his colleagues were at a loss to explain.

為什麼人類始終如此在意對方的膚色，這點也使他大惑不解。

解析

就從名詞 loss 著手吧，它的本意是「損／喪失」，用在片語 at a loss 裡，指人「茫然若失，不知所措」的感覺。這個片語的後面常跟著不定詞 (to V)，就如以上的英譯，也可以接 for 這個介詞。「我不知道該怎麼正確回應／答。」英文可以表示為：I was at a loss for an appropriate reply.

> **小試身手**
>
> 16. 當老師問她這題怎麼答，她根本不會。
>
> _____

（17）flow on and on 滔滔不絕；流個不停（19段）

As the alien's stream of analysis flowed on and on, a hush fell over the room.

外星人滔滔不絕的言論，使我們整個大廳鴉雀無聲。

解析

動詞 flow 指的是液體或氣體的「流動」，之後所跟的 on and on 其實是副詞，給人的感覺是「持續不停地」、「不斷向前地」。因而整個片語當然給人的感覺就是「不停歇地向前流動」，如果拿來形容人說話，就是「滔滔不絕，說個沒完沒了」的意思。

小試身手

17. 他就站在那裡，望著河水奔流。

_____

（18）be an authority on... 為（某方面的）權威（20段）

Because he was an authority on the subject, he had been invited to speak.

由於他是此方面的權威，所以也就常被請去發表論文。

解析

an authority 指的是「權威（人物）」，中文習慣上把「人物」兩個字略掉，留下權威兩字，事實上還是指人。讀者們只要記得後面跟著 on 這個介詞以表示「某領域的權威人物」。

小試身手

18. 她是很受敬重的中美外交史權威。

_____

(19) given... 給⋯⋯（22段）

His theory was that given enough time, humans would eventually become like other animals: they would cease fighting wars and stop abusing their own kind.

他的理論是，只要假以時日，人類也會像其他動物一樣，不再有戰爭，也不再虐待自己的同類。

解析

把 given... 選列為重點，倒不是它具有什麼不得了的意義，而是它的用法。given... 是一種固定的、習慣性的用法，基本上用以表示一種假定性的狀況，可以看成是 if 子句的精簡形態。各位不覺得其實英譯裡的 given enough time 事實上就是 if they were given enough time 這個副詞子句的精簡形態嗎？從字面看，相當於中文「如果給人類足夠時間」，也是原著裡的「假以時日」，譯者以 given enough time 處理，夠傳神吧！

> **小試身手**
>
> 19. 在天氣寒冷的情況下，我很擔心他們的表現會不如我們所預期。
>
> _____

(20) remind someone of something 令某人想起某事（25段）

It reminded me of what the alien had said, and it also made me think of a quote I had learned in elementary school: "Man is the soul of the universe."

（它）讓我想起外星人的話，卻也想起我小學的時候就學會的一句話，「人是萬物之靈」。

解析

remind 的本意是「提醒⋯⋯」、「使⋯⋯想起」，很自然地後面常以某人為受

詞。比如英譯裡的 it reminded me 就是「讓我想起」，而如果你想表達「使某人想起」當然就是以 something reminds someone 來表示。這應該不成問題吧，接下來讀者要把重點擺在介詞 of。到底「讓我想起（什麼）」「使某人想起（什麼）」？我們就得在這個（什麼）之前加上介詞 of 才算功德圓滿。請利用以下練習，讓學習更加圓滿。

小試身手

20. 佛洛斯特寫的這首詩讓我想起李白寫的一首中國名詩。

_____

小試身手解答

1. Experts on pollution control were sent for from all over the world.

2. It is next to impossible to ride a bicycle from Taipei to Kaohsiung in a day.

3. They decided to run more tests on the software before marketing it.

4-1. If you have nothing better to do, go do the dishes.

4-2. Having nothing better to do, I switched on my computer and began to play some video games, just to kill time.

5. I broke out in a cold sweat as the sound of stomping feet came nearer and nearer.

6-1. Where did she say she wanted to be picked up?

6-2. I picked up some Spanish during my stay in Argentine.

6-3. I was then in a remote part of the mountains and my cell phone couldn't pick up any signal.

7-1. My travels often take me a great distance(away)from home.

7-2. The advent of modern jet airliners has made it a short distance to fly from New York to L.A.

7-3. This picture can only be fully appreciated at a certain distance.

8. The satellite is sent up to spy on the enemy's military activities.

9. He shut himself in the laboratory and focused all his time and energy on discovering that mysterious material.

10. I know I need to do more research to gain a better/deeper understanding of the phenomenon.

11. The answers listed below are for reference purposes only.

12. Despite having faith in her, I found myself worrying anyway.

13. Even today, the theory of relativity is incomprehensible to most people.

14. The protesters accuse the WTO of exploiting the poor under the pretext of promoting free trade. (或 using free trade as a pretext to exploit the poor.)

15. He further expressed confusion at how they budgeted and spent the money.

16. When the teacher asked her how to solve the problem, she was completely at a loss.

17. He just stood there, watching the river flow on and on.

18. She is highly regarded as an authority on Sino-American diplomatic history.

19. I'm afraid that given the chilly weather, their performance might not be up to our expectations.

20. This poem by Frost reminds me of a famous Chinese piece by Li Bai.

Linking English
讀李家同學英文4：竊聽者

2007年10月初版　　　　　　　　　　　定價：新臺幣250元
2016年6月初版第二刷
有著作權・翻印必究
Printed in Taiwan.

著　　　者	李　家　同
譯　　　者	Nick Hawkins
解　　　析	周　正　一
總　編　輯	胡　金　倫
總　經　理	羅　國　俊
發　行　人	林　載　爵

出　版　者	聯經出版事業股份有限公司	叢書主編　何　采　嬪
地　　　址	台北市基隆路一段180號4樓	校　　對　Nick Hawkins
台北聯經書房	台北市新生南路三段94號	林　慧　如
電　　　話	(0 2) 2 3 6 2 0 3 0 8	封面設計　翁　國　鈞
台中分公司	台中市北區崇德路一段198號	
暨門市電話	(0 4) 2 2 3 1 2 0 2 3	
郵政劃撥帳戶第 0 1 0 0 5 5 9 - 3 號		
郵撥電話	(0 2) 2 3 6 2 0 3 0 8	
印　刷　者	文聯彩色製版印刷有限公司	
總　經　銷	聯合發行股份有限公司	
發　行　所	新北市新店區寶橋路235巷6弄6號2F	
電　　　話	(0 2) 2 9 1 7 8 0 2 2	

行政院新聞局出版事業登記證局版臺業字第0130號

本書如有缺頁，破損，倒裝請寄回台北聯經書房更換。　　ISBN　978-957-08-3201-3 (平裝)
聯經網址 http://www.linkingbooks.com.tw
電子信箱 e-mail:linking@udngroup.com

國家圖書館出版品預行編目資料

讀李家同學英文 4：竊聽者 /
李家同著 . Nick Hawkins 譯 . 周正一解析 .
初版 . 臺北市：聯經，2007 年（民 96）
240 面；14.8×21 公分 .（Linking English）
ISBN 978-957-08-3201-3（平裝附光碟）
[2016 年 6 月初版第二刷]

1.英語　2.讀本

805.18　　　　　　　　　　96018441